Aussie

STEM Stars

EMMA JOHNSTON

Marine biologist and TV presenter

Aussie

STEM Stars

EMMA JOHNSTON

Marine biologist and TV presenter

Story told by DEE WHITE

Aussie STEM Stars series
Published by Wild Dingo Press
Melbourne, Australia
books@wilddingopress.com.au
wilddingopress.com.au

This work was first published by Wild Dingo Press 2022

Cover Design: Gisela Beer
Illustrations: Mirjana Segan
Series Editor: Catherine Lewis
Printed in Australia.

White, Dee 1964-, author.
Emma Johnston: Marine biologist and TV presenter

A catalogue record for this
book is available from the
National Library of Australia

ISBN: 9781925893762 (paperback)
ISBN: 9781925893267 (epdf)
ISBN: 9781925893601 (epub)

When you're facing a challenge,
trust the people who say you're up for it
and let their support carry you forward.

– Emma Johnston

Disclaimer

This book has been developed in collaboration with Professor Emma Johnston AO FTSE FRSN. Names have been changed and many fictional elements introduced for narrative flow.

Contents

1

1983: The darkness

Emma stared out of her classroom window. She hated being stuck inside on days like this, when it was so hot that her dress clung to her legs and her feet sweated inside her school shoes. She longed to be at the beach, running through the shallows feeling the wet sand between her toes then diving headfirst into the cool blue water. Sometimes she wondered what it would be like to be a fish and get to spend all day in the ocean.

'Emma, are you paying attention?' asked Mrs Green.

Emma liked her teacher and most of the time she liked school, just not when it was so hot, and not when they were doing maths that bored her. Emma had always loved maths almost as much as she loved the beach. She loved the way numbers could fit so neatly together and the way they could be used to work out things in real life like the area of the oval that she ran around at lunchtime.

But Emma's love for maths had waned recently because she wasn't learning anything new. She knew her times tables by heart, up to fifteen, and how to round out decimals and convert them to fractions. Emma wanted more complicated problems like the ones Dad gave her at home. Problems like working out the wind speed when she and her older brother, Ben, were racing their sailing boat, or how much water there was in Grandpa's fish tank.

Emma wished she were racing their boat right now, feeling the refreshing sea breeze on her face.

'Emma, are you paying attention?' Her teacher repeated.

'No, Mrs Green. Sorry, Mrs Green,' Emma said.

Mrs Green's smile was kind. 'I know it's hard to concentrate in this heat.'

Emma held up her exercise book. 'I've finished all my work.'

Mrs Green scanned the pages. 'Well done. We'll have to find you more to do.'

Emma didn't want more work, she wanted more interesting work.

'Smarty pants,' Her friend, Bruce, leaned over to look at her maths sheet, every answer with a neat tick beside it.

She glanced at his half-finished work. 'Would you like some help?'

He nodded, 'Thanks.'

Emma showed Bruce how to add and subtract the five and six-digit numbers on the worksheets. Mrs Green had shown them already, but instructions just didn't seem to stick in Bruce's head, and Emma didn't want her friend to get into trouble for not finishing his work. Emma's Dad was a mathematician and he had shown her how to do these problems years ago.

Bruce went on with his work and Mrs Green came back with a new maths sheet. 'That should keep you busy till the end of the day, Emma,' she said.

Emma glanced up at the clock. Thankfully, it was almost home time. When she looked at the new maths sheet, she groaned. The problems were exactly the same kind as the ones she'd just completed so easily. She turned back to the window. At first she thought it was her imagination, but the sky seemed to be getting darker. Then she noticed her nose and throat felt dry. She walked down to the front of the class where Mrs Green was marking other students' work. 'Can I get a drink please?' She asked.

'There's only half an hour till the bell. I'm sure you can wait,' her teacher replied.

Emma went back to her seat and stared out the window again. It was definitely getting darker outside and the wind was picking up. It seemed as if the sky were a huge black cloud rushing towards them.

Dust swept in through the open windows and kids started coughing. Mrs Green looked up. 'Mrs Green, what's happening?' Emma could hardly get the words out. The sky was almost completely black.

Everyone stopped working to stare at the sky closing in on them. Mrs Green rushed over and shut the windows, but she didn't respond to Emma's question. Perhaps she didn't know why the sky had turned dark either.

Kids rushed to the windows and jostled for the best view. From her seat, Emma didn't need to move to see what was happening.

'It's an alien spaceship come to take us to Mars,' said Bruce.

Emma didn't think so, but she almost hoped it was. She had a sick feeling in her stomach and was glad that Mrs Green had closed the windows. What if it were a nuclear dust cloud?

At home her parents talked a lot about the **Cold War** between the **USSR** (dominated by Russia) and America and how both sides wanted to be the country with the most nuclear weapons. And Emma had seen it spoken about on the news. Her parents had even talked about the possibility of war. Perhaps this was it. Perhaps the world was at war.

Emma tried to push the fear down, to make it go away. She didn't want to scare her friends, so she kept her thoughts to herself. But Amos Stafford was clearly thinking the same thing. He blurted out, 'It's a nuclear war, for sure'.

'Of course, it's not,' Mrs Green hastened to reassure them, but Emma wasn't convinced.

Kids started screaming. Mrs Green banged the blackboard with her duster and called for calm. Inside the classroom it was thick with fear. Although some children stayed by the window peering out, others hid under their desks.

'Everything's fine. Back to your seats, everyone,' said Mrs Green, but Emma heard the quiver in her voice and knew that their teacher was scared too.

It was so dark outside now that Emma couldn't even see the trees across the street, but an electricity pole in front of the school was being buffeted by the wind. The silent blackness had been scary enough, but what happened next was even more frightening.

The world outside the school was suddenly full of noise with the cracking of tree branches and sirens of emergency vehicles as they screamed past. Emma held her breath, expecting armed soldiers to burst through the door at any moment. She felt sure that Australia was at war.

Mrs Green hurried to lock the classroom door.

'It's perfectly safe in here,' she assured them.

Then the electricity pole that had been blowing around out the front of the school toppled to the ground. Sparks flew through the blackness. Even Emma screamed then. The smell and taste of dust on her tongue was almost as stifling as the heat. The classroom was so stuffy with all the windows closed and Emma wished she'd been allowed to get that drink of water. The bubble taps were just outside, so close, but beyond her reach.

The smell of the dust made her think about the abandoned house down the road. It was falling down and they weren't supposed to go there, but it was such a fun place to explore. Emma's little brother Sam said he saw a ghost sitting on the front step once, but Emma didn't believe in things that there was no scientific explanation for.

Emma was fascinated by the world around her and at home, her questions were always answered. Her mother had been forced to give up her career as a scientist after Sam was born and she became an artist instead, but she was always happy to explain to her children about how things worked. Emma knew from Mum about the moon's influence on the tides, how to read a weather map and why we can see colours. Emma wondered what her mother's explanation for this blackness would be.

Thinking about her brother, Sam, and his 'ghost' made Emma even more anxious. Sam had only just started school. He would be terrified, wondering what was happening outside too. Emma hurried up the front to her teacher.

'Can I please go and find my little brother? He's only in prep and he'll be very scared. He needs me.' Her voice went high and she could feel tears prick the back of her eyelids as she pictured Sam's frightened face.

Mrs Green shook her head. 'I'm afraid nobody can leave the classroom. It's too dangerous. Don't worry, his teacher will take care of him.'

'But…' Emma's lip quivered. She gulped back a sob.

'I'm sorry, Emma, I know you're worried, but it's perfectly safe in here. We must all stay where we are until it passes.'

Nobody seemed to know what 'it' was. Emma hoped she was wrong about 'it' being related to the Cold War. She'd always thought Australia was a safe place to live, but now she wasn't so sure.

2

Nature's way

It took more than half an hour for the blackness to clear, drifting off like a silent shadow, leaving destruction and chaos behind. Nobody in the classroom moved at first. Emma wondered how changed the world outside her classroom would be.

Nobody seemed to know what had just happened. Would Emma's house still be standing, would the beach that she loved so much still be there or would the sand have been blown away with the cloud that had turned everything to darkness?

Out the front of the school, tree branches had been snapped clean off and the letterbox across the road had been torn from its post. Emma was glad now that they had taken shelter in the classroom, but she worried about both her brothers. It was past the end of school time and Emma was keen to go in search of Ben and Sam.

Everyone headed for the classroom door like a swarm of bees, but Mrs Green refused to open it.

'You can't all just run outside. It's still dangerous out there. A power pole has fallen down out the front of the school so we all need to leave calmly by the back entrance.'

The fallen pole was the one that Emma had seen tumble to the ground, sending sparks flying. She knew about electricity and the risks of being electrocuted. Mum had explained to them all about how electricity worked. So, she was happy to do what Mrs Green said. The teacher organised the children into single file and directed them out through the back door onto the school oval.

Emma was glad to be out of the stuffy classroom, but it wasn't much better outside. It was still sweltering hot, her eyes stung and her skin had turned a reddy brown. Everything seemed to be covered in dust and the air was choked with it. Emma's throat was parched but she didn't have time to stop for a drink. Sam and Ben were out there somewhere waiting for her. She looked for them in the sea of kids but in school uniform everyone looked alike.

The students were organised into year level groups and the oval was ringed with anxious parents waiting to pick up their children.

Emma and her brothers normally walked home alone, but today Mum was there to meet them.

The principal spoke, wishing everyone a safe journey home and then dismissed each year level one by one. The preps were first and when Emma saw Sam run to Mum, she gasped with relief. Her little brother was safe. She wanted to run and hug him, but she had to wait for her grade to be released.

Dust-covered kids embraced dust-covered parents. Emma couldn't wait to get home and scrub herself clean. The dust was everywhere. In her eyes, her nose, her ears, her mouth, the pocket of her dress and even her school bag. She had thought that nuclear fallout would look and smell different.

The sky was red like the dust, but she couldn't see soldiers or weapons of any kind. Perhaps this wasn't a war.

When Emma's year level was called, she was one of the first to bolt across the oval. Mum was so always so calm and practical so it surprised Emma to see a tear in the corner of her eye as they hugged.

'That was some dust storm,' Mum said.

'Was it nuclear dust?' The words felt clogged in Emma's throat. Ben nodded and Emma was sure he was about to ask the same question.

Mum smiled. 'No, this had nothing to do with a nuclear war.' She shook her head. 'It's part of nature's war against humans.'

'What do you mean?' asked Emma.

'If we don't look after the environment, these kinds of things will continue to happen – and worse.'

As they walked home, they took it in turns to piggyback Sam who behaved like royalty, waving and smiling at everyone they passed.

Mum explained that scientists had predicted events like this, but people didn't listen.

'The dust was topsoil blown all the way from the Mallee, 500 kilometres away,' she said.

Emma couldn't even imagine how far that was, but it seemed a very long way.

'Why did the topsoil blow away?' She asked.

'Freaky wind conditions,' said Ben. 'My turn.' He reached to take Sam from Emma's shoulders.

'That's true,' said Mum. 'But that's only part of it. It also happened because the land in the Mallee has been eroded and degraded by farming.'

Emma couldn't understand how farming the land could have caused what just happened. Farmers grew food for them to eat. Wasn't that a good thing?

'The ground used to be covered by native vegetation that didn't need much water,' said Mum. 'So even when there was a drought, the vegetation still grew and was able to anchor the soil in place.'

'What happened to the anchor plants?' asked Emma.

'When the farmers took over the land they got rid of them and planted their own crops. But the things they planted died when the drought came because they couldn't survive without a lot of water. When the crops died, there was nothing to hold the soil in place, so it blew away – all the way to Melbourne.'

Emma was glad that the dust storm hadn't been caused by a nuclear war, but she was worried about what would happen to the land where the soil had blown away.

'It will take a very long time to recover,' said Mum. She frowned. 'And it's not just a vegetation problem. The chemicals used on the farms have been washed away with the soil into the rivers and creeks, and that causes animals and plant life to get sick and even die.'

'Can't they stop using chemicals?' asked Emma. She hated to think of the fish and frogs dying because people were poisoning the water. She wondered if the same thing happened to the creatures living in the sea.

Mum told her that they suffered from pollution too.

'And not just from chemicals. People leave their rubbish lying on the beaches and it washes into the sea and animals get caught in it and die.'

Emma was horrified to learn that such terrible things could happen to the ocean she loved so much and the animals and plants living in it.

Sam was almost asleep on Ben's shoulders by the time they got home and Emma was tired too.

She was relieved to see the house still standing, even if it was a little dirtier than it was when she left for school that morning.

Dad was late home from work that night because the strong winds had blown a signal across the train track. On the news, Emma saw how a man had to swim to safety after his boat capsized in the freak storm. Emma shuddered as she thought how scary the whole thing had been, and of the wrecked land in the Mallee, and the damage that people were doing to life in the oceans and rivers.

That night as they sat around the dinner table, they talked about how lucky they were to have all come out of the storm unscathed. She was so grateful to have her family around her. But Emma couldn't stop thinking about the fish and animal families broken apart and killed by the actions of people.

3

Setting sail

Memories of the dust storm stayed with Emma for a long time. She remembered how scared she'd been as she watched branches ripped from trees and daylight turned to darkness. She remembered how it felt to see debris caught by the storm and dumped on her beloved beach. She and her family had helped with the clean-up. So many boats had been damaged in the storm but luckily, theirs was stored undercover at the boathouse.

Emma loved boats and sailing. She loved the silence of the sea. She loved being in touch with the wind and feeling it carry her forward. She and her older brother, Ben, had been racing together for quite a few years now, and with Ben's cunning and Emma's determination they made a formidable team.

Emma tucked her brown hair under her cap and applied a thick layer of sunscreen. She couldn't wait to be out on the boat with sea birds circling overhead. Sailing made her feel wild and free.

Her sharp mind loved the strategy in boating, particularly racing. Just by the way they positioned and moved the sails, Emma and Ben could control how their boat moved through the water. They had been on boats since they were babies and they were strong swimmers. As soon as they were old enough to understand, Mum and Dad had taught them how to sail; how to fly the main sail, jib and spinnaker.

Although Emma was two years younger than her brother, she was a quick learner and very competitive. Racing excited her.

'You come from a long line of sea people,' said Dad. 'Your grandpa used to walk through the shallows of this beach with his battery torch during the depression, spearing flounder to feed himself and his siblings.

'Are there any pirates in our family?' asked Emma. A pirate's life seemed so wild and free.

'Mum laughed. 'Yes, some of your ancestors in Scotland were pirates of a sort. They had a castle on a rocky coast and would row their boats out to steal from the passing ships. We also have sailors and swimmers and even a lighthouse keeper in our ancestry. Dad's right, a love of the sea runs in the family.'

Now Emma understood why she was drawn to the sea.

She and Ben had started out racing a mirror, a small, light boat that was easy to transport and hard to capsize – the perfect craft for beginners. Their skills had developed and when Emma was in Year 7 they began racing a Kitty Cat, a catamaran with two hulls and a spinnaker. It was much faster than the mirror. Their boat was called *Nereus* after a sea god in ancient mythology.

Races always took place on Saturday afternoon, and today, Emma and Ben were feeling pumped. After the dust storm had cleared, everything was so much brighter and the air seemed fresher.

'I really want to win today,' said Emma. Sailing always put her in a good mood.

Ben grinned. 'Me too.'

Sam, Mum and Dad helped Emma and Ben set up for the race. It took four people to jiggle the Kitty Cat out of the rack in the boatshed. They carried her to the trolley and wheeled her past the other boats. Emma recognised one of the other competitors, Jack Lynley from Ben's year at school. His craft, *Titan*, was newer and sleeker than theirs and had cost a lot more money. Jack liked to give them a hard time about their boat.

As they carried *Nereus* past him, Jack said to his brother, loud enough for everyone to hear. 'The Johnstons are racing that fruit box again. They'll never win.'

'Did you hear that?' Emma could feel herself getting hot with anger.

'We'll just have to show them,' said Ben.

Jack's comment made Emma even more determined. It took more than the most expensive boat to win a race. Emma and Ben won often because of their skill and teamwork. It never seemed to matter that their boat wasn't the best one in the race. Ben was smart and Emma trusted his judgement most of the time.

'I'd hate to be Jack's crew,' she said. 'It'd be hard to get past his big head. There's not much room on a boat. I'd probably get forced overboard.'

Ben laughed.

'Just ignore him,' said Mum. 'Your Dad and I get those kinds of comments when we race too. But they don't have so much to say when we win,' she grinned.

Together Ben and Emma rigged the Kitty Cat for the race. Mum and Dad helped them lift *Nereus* up and carry the boat to the water's edge.

'Good luck,' said Mum.

'You can do this,' said Dad.

'I bet you win,' said Sam.

'Aww, thanks, Sam.' Emma hugged her little brother.

Excited but focused, Ben and Emma faced the Kitty Cat into the waves, waded out into the water and hoisted themselves up onto the boat. There wasn't much room to stand on the hull of *Nereus* and the wind was picking up as they climbed on board. Emma almost lost her balance and put her hands out just in time to stop herself from being washed into the choppy seas. That was a close call.

She grinned as she refocused her attention on what they needed to do.

'This is good weather for us, right?'

Ben nodded. 'Strong winds are better for heavier craft like ours.

Both safely on board, they slipped on their harnesses and made their way towards the start of the race. Ben licked his finger and held it up to the wind. He confirmed the wind direction with the indicator on their boat's mast.

As per usual, Emma's tummy was in knots before a race. So many things could go wrong and although she loved the sea, she was also aware of its dangers. She was always nervous before a race, but as soon as it started she became focused and her tummy settled down.

They pointed *Nereus* into the wind and jostled with the other competitors for the best position at the starting line. Ben checked his watch.

'We need to hang back a bit. We need to time it perfectly so we cross the starting line in the best position.'

Emma glanced at the shore. It was far away but she imagined she could see Mum, Dad and Sam waving and cheering them on. Imagining her family there supporting her, helped her to relax.

She got distracted thinking about them and suddenly, *Titan*, skippered by Jack Lynley burst through between the boats.

Not missing an opportunity, Jack called out, 'Told you we'd thrash you.'

Emma felt as though she'd let Ben down.

'Sorry, I wasn't paying attention,' she said. All around them voices were shouting, 'port' and 'starboard' as the Kitty Cats jostled for prime position, almost crashing into each other.

'No need to be sorry,' said Ben. 'Look!' He pointed to *Titan* which had gone over the starting line before the starting gun had fired. Emma couldn't help smiling as the sleek-looking Kitty Cat was sent back around all the other boats to approach the start again.

Emma watched the starter closely. She didn't want that happening to them. Finally, the gun went off and they were away.

Emma and Ben went out hard, trying to sail as close to the wind as possible to build up speed.

'You're doing great, Em,' Ben encouraged.

But *Titan* was lighter and faster. It passed them and hit the lead.

'Losers!' Jack called out.

Emma struggled to hide her disappointment. After such a great start, she couldn't believe that the race was slipping out of their hands.'

'It's not over yet. You'll see.' Ben grinned.

They trimmed the sails, trying to get as much lift and forward motion as they could.

'We need to catch Jack before we go around the buoy,' said Ben.

The skipper of the boat behind yelled out for them to get out of the way, but Ben and Emma stuck to their course. They were way ahead and not prepared to lose ground. They went up on one hull, trying to get maximum lift.

To stop *Nereus* from capsizing, Emma leapt to the outer side. She was thumped by the waves, but she clung on. The water was freezing but Emma held on tight.

'Tack.' Ben spoke softly so that only Emma would hear. It was one of his tactics, to keep their plans to themselves and take the other competitors by surprise.

They turned into the wind. It was starting to build up just as Ben had anticipated. Emma and Ben had known these waters of Port Phillip Bay from birth.

Ahead they could see that *Titan* was being buffeted about by the wind and the crew were doing everything they could to stay on course.

Soon, Emma and Ben had overtaken *Titan* and started to turn the boat around the buoy. As they turned, Emma almost flew under the boom, making sure it didn't hit her on the head as she made the leap. She pulled out the sail and jumped out onto the other side of the boat. It was a seamless manoeuvre, one they'd done together many times before.

Titan was closing the gap from behind but didn't have enough room to catch *Nereus* and her fierce competitors before they crossed the finish line first.

When they returned to shore, Mum, Dad and Sam rushed to congratulate them. The only thing souring the victory for Emma was that Ben received a handsome pewter mug while she was given a flimsy silver vase with flowers on it. She was the only girl sailing Kitty Cats and didn't like being reminded of it.

4

Animals can surprise you

Emma had always wanted a dog. She loved the idea of taking it to the beach with her, throwing frisbees to it on the sand, maybe even taking it sailing. Some of the people she saw out on the water had dogs on board. But the family travelled a lot with Dad's work and her parents said that it wouldn't be fair on the dog if they had to re home it every time they went away.

Instead, the family kept budgerigars, quails and fish – pets that grandparents could easily take care of while Emma and her family travelled. Mum and Dad built a large aviary out the back for the budgies, under the trees so they would have shade in summer.

Emma loved to sit and watch the lively birds fly about, splashes of colour in the speckled light. She loved the cheerful sounds they made as they greeted and groomed each other.

Emma and her brothers were responsible for looking after their pets. Every day, they filled the seed bins in the aviary with food and made sure the birds had fresh water. They gave them shell grit and other things that wild birds would normally eat to help their digestive systems.

The aviary was covered with dry sand and leaves so it was just like a forest floor and Emma loved to watch the little quails forage in it and dust bathe in the sand. They were so funny the way their sharp little feet kicking grains everywhere, and they scratched for their food like chickens.

The quails didn't seem to be bothered at all by the budgies who were very active, constantly flying from one end of the aviary to the other. Emma had read that budgies were smart, and in the wild, often travelled long distances in search of food.

To stop them from getting bored, Emma and her brothers gave them a variety of toys. Sometimes, they pecked at the wood and used it to keep their beaks trimmed. One of the budgies' favourite toys was a swing with a disc on the bottom for them to chew. They also loved making the silver bell in the aviary tinkle and looking at themselves in a mirror wired to the side.

Mum made a nesting box and two of the budgies bred. Five eggs became five fluffy baby birds that Emma could hold in the palms of her hands.

Her favourite budgie was Simon. He lived inside and Emma carried him all over the house on her shoulder like a pirate. She tried to teach him to talk, repeating words to him over and over again, but he only ever learned to say, 'Hello, Simon'.

Simon was very affectionate and as he rode around on Emma's shoulder he would often bend and nuzzle her cheek with his head. He liked to roost on doors, tucking his head into his wings and holding on with his feet.

The family also had goldfish which kept Emma fascinated for hours. It calmed her to watch them swimming around, swishing their tails gracefully as they moved silently through the water.

'I don't understand how you can spend so long watching fish,' said her friend, Holly. 'They're so boring.'

'No, they're not,' said Emma. 'Look how Billy's chasing Patch and Sunshine is keeping out of the way.'

'How can you even tell them apart?' asked Holly.

'Billy's the bright orange one. Sunshine is pale yellow, and Patch has black squares on his tail.'

Holly shrugged. 'They all look the same to me.'

'They're not,' said Emma. She beckoned Holly over to the mirror and they stood side by side. 'See how different we are. Fish are like us. They come in all shapes and sizes and they have different personalities, just like people. Billy likes to chase the other fish, but Sunshine likes to hide away in the corner.'

Holly scratched her head. 'They're not very smart though. Imagine having a three-second memory. You wouldn't even remember your own name.'

Emma laughed. 'That's totally not true. Fish are way smarter than that and they remember things for a lot longer than three seconds. Watch this.'

When Emma walked up to the tank, the fish swam to the top right-hand corner straightaway.

'What did you do?' asked Holly.

'Nothing. They know me and they remember that's where I feed them. And last time I fed them was hours ago. See, smarter than you think!' Emma grinned.

5

Off to Japan

Emma was sitting at the dining table with Simon perched on her shoulder, her feet tapping on the wooden floor. Even Simon seemed to sense the importance of the occasion. He bobbed up and down and squawked, 'Hello, Simon'.

Emma and her brothers sat in a line, watching their parents, wondering why a family meeting had been called.

Mum grinned at them. 'Don't look so worried. It's good news.'

Dad nodded. 'I've been offered a position in Japan.'

'And we've decided to take it,' said Mum.

Japan, that was a long way away.

'Do they have beaches over there?' Emma asked.

Mum laughed. 'Of course, they do. It's an island, just like Australia.'

'But for starters, we'll be stationed in Tokyo,' said Dad.

'Cool! They have a Disneyland in Tokyo.' Ben's face lit up.

Emma still wasn't sure about going to Japan. She'd been looking forward to Grade Six and being head of the school.

'How long will we be there for?' She asked.

'About a year,' Dad replied.

'But what about school?' said Emma.

'They have schools in Japan. Good schools,' said Mum. 'I've heard their maths and science programs are way ahead of ours.' Mum put her arm on Emma's shoulder. 'You might even like it better over there.'

Emma wondered if she might too. She was ready to be challenged more at maths and science. But she still wondered what it would be like in Japan. Everything would be different. She remembered back to when they lived in France a few years ago and she felt like an outsider at first, until she learnt French, and broke her arm, and all the kids wanted to write on her plaster and look after her.

'Do they speak English in Japan?' she asked.

Mum nodded. 'Some people do, but not everyone. School is taught in Japanese.'

'Japanese?' said Ben.

'Don't worry,' said Dad. 'You'll soon pick it up.'

Emma was determined to. She made up her mind to start learning Japanese straightaway.

Simon rubbed his head gently against Emma's ear as if to say, 'What about me?' Emma wasn't sure that Simon would like Japan. She wasn't even sure if she would. 'What about Simon and the other budgies? What about the fish? Will they come too?'

Mum shook her head. 'Grandma and Grandpa will look after them for us.'

Simon nuzzled his head against Emma's. 'I'll miss you.' she whispered.

'What about our friends?' asked Sam.

'It's only for a year. You'll make friends in Japan.'

Emma would miss her friends too, especially Holly. They'd been friends since they were born.

But she was excited about their new adventure, excited to be going to Japan.

They'd been on lots of camping trips, but it was hard to know what to pack when you were going to be away for 12 months. And they had to include things like slip on shoes because in Japan everyone took off their shoes to go into temples, homes and even restaurants. Mum also suggested that Emma pack warm pyjamas.

'Even though it's summer here, we'll be arriving in winter because Japan is in the northern hemisphere. It'll be cold there at night,' she said.

They'd all been reading books to learn about Japanese life and customs too, and Emma had discovered that if you handed someone a present, you had to do it with both hands, and that it would be received in the same way. She'd packed some Australian souvenirs to give to new friends she made in Japan.

As they loaded their suitcases into the car, Emma had forgotten her trepidation about going to Japan. Her tummy buzzed with excitement at the thought of flying.

At the airport, Dad stacked their suitcases on a trolley and pushed it through the front door to the check-in counter. They showed their tickets to a woman in a smart blue uniform and pushed their luggage onto a moving conveyor belt that whisked it away.

While they waited to board their plane, Emma and her brothers lined up at the window and watched the other planes leaving and coming in to land. Emma loved the way they floated above the runway like giant birds. She was excited to be given the window seat for take-off, although she promised to swap with Ben and Sam during the nine-hour flight to Japan.

Emma peered out the window of the plane at its huge wing. 'How do airplanes fly?' She asked.

'With their wings.' Ben grinned.

'I know that, but they're so big and heavy.'

'Look at the shape of their wings,' said Mum. 'See how they're curved on top and flat on the bottom. They're specially designed so that the air moving along them holds them up.'

'They generate a force called lift,' said Dad.

Mum handed them each a lolly to suck on during take-off.

'It'll stop your ears from popping,' she said.

The air pressure changes suddenly inside a plane when it takes off. When you suck on a lolly and swallow, it helps make the pressure inside your ears the same as the pressure around you.

The wheels of the plane rumbled along the runway as the aircraft built up speed. Emma's stomach jolted as they rose into the air. She stared out the window. The wing flaps on the plane had folded back down again. Below them, the cars, trees and houses got smaller and smaller. Soon they were high in the sky and the clouds outside the window looked like fluffy cotton wool balls.

'I wish I could touch them,' said Emma. 'They look so soft.'

Mum laughed. 'They wouldn't feel soft if you touched them – they'd feel wet.'

'Why?' asked Emma.

'They're made of water drops so your hand would go straight through them.'

Soon they were flying high above the clouds. The sky went dark and there was nothing to see except the twinkling plane lights on the end of the wings.

They landed on the runway in Tokyo, the capital of Japan, with a bump. They emerged yawning from the plane as they stretched their arms and legs, then headed to the carousel to collect their luggage.

Emma and her brothers had learnt some Japanese, but she was relieved to see that most of the signs were written in English as well. She had read that there were ten museums in Tokyo and she couldn't wait to visit every single one of them.

All around them people were speaking Japanese. They talked so fast that Emma couldn't understand what they were saying. It made her feel strange, as if she were being left out of something important. It was the same way she had felt when they went to live in France and she didn't speak French. But it hadn't taken her long to feel like she belonged. In France, Emma had learnt to understand what people were saying by reading their facial expressions and body language when she couldn't read their words.

After they had collected their bags from the carousel, they hurried to the exit where a man with dark hair and a serious face stood holding up a sign with JOHNSTON FAMILY written on it. Mum spoke to him in Japanese and did the introductions. The man's name was Haruto. He told them that his name meant, 'to soar or fly'.

Haruto opened the car doors so they could pile in.

'I'm glad I'm not driving,' said Dad.

There were more cars on the streets of Tokyo than Emma had ever seen in her life. They passed tall buildings and footpaths overflowing with people. Haruto stopped outside an apartment block with people everywhere.

'This is one of the busiest parts of Tokyo,' he explained.

All of Tokyo looked busy to Emma.

Haruto helped them get their luggage out of the car and check in. Then they took the lift to their apartment. It was bigger than the one in Grenoble in France, but still small for a family of five. Emma liked the paintings on the walls. There was one of a butterfly koi that looked just like one of their goldfish back home.

'I'm hungry,' said Sam.

'Me too,' Emma and Ben chimed in.

Mum grinned. 'We can unpack later. Let's go and find food.'

Outside it was still so crowded with people that it was hard to walk. The family stuck close together so that nobody got lost. There were no fish and chip shops or milk bars. But they found a sushi bar and Emma tasted sushi for the first time. It was different, but delicious. Hardly anyone seemed to speak English, but everyone smiled a lot, especially at the children. Everyone seemed to be in such a hurry in Japan, but Emma wanted to take her time and look at everything, at the skyscrapers and historic temples. It was all so new and different

from their home in Williamstown. The streets were full of red and white buses crowded with people, and wide pedestrian walkways.

Dad took them to the **Shibuya Crossing**, near the Shibuya station. It was the biggest pedestrian crossing Emma had ever seen.

'When I'm not working, we'll catch the train from Shibuya station and go exploring,' Dad said.

Emma couldn't wait.

6

Sensei and science

It took them a while to settle into Tokyo life, to get used to living in a cramped two-bedroom apartment in a high-rise building, but Emma loved sharing a room with her brothers and chatting every night about their new life in Japan.

There were 500 children at her new primary school and she and Sam were the only non-Japanese students. Emma's Japanese language skills were still very poor and nobody at the school seemed to speak English.

The classroom was huge with a big rectangle blackboard on the front wall and there were more than forty students in the class. Each student had a small table and a hard wooden chair. Emma chose a seat on the side, near the window where she wouldn't feel so conspicuous. Students smiled at her as they passed, and she smiled back. Everyone seemed friendly, even if she didn't know what they were saying.

The blackboard was surrounded by notices, all written in Japanese so that Emma couldn't read them.

The first lesson was history. She recognised that word, but not much else about the lesson. She tried to work out what the teacher was saying from her **non-verbal cues**, but often the teacher turned away from her to face the other side of the classroom. The students showed great respect for their teacher and called her, Sensei.

Non-verbal cues
Messages and information passed on without using words through eye contact, facial expressions, gestures, posture and the distance between two people.

Emma watched and tried hard to work out what was being said, but she barely understood a word. She found herself losing concentration and staring out the window or at the clock and then calculating how much time till the bell rang. She watched the second hand tick over on the clock. The morning dragged.

But at lunchtime, the language barrier didn't matter. Everyone was playing games that anyone could be part of. Emma and Sam joined in tag, a game played by children all over the world, even if the rules differed slightly.

After lunch they did maths and science. Emma didn't need good Japanese language skills to understand and love what was happening in these classes. Sensei used practical experiments to demonstrate the principles to the class and Emma could learn just by watching, looking at the diagrams, and applying the knowledge she had already.

Sensei filled a glass container with water and dropped ice blocks into it, then placed strings across the top of the ice. She sprinkled the ice blocks with salt and when she picked up the string, the ice blocks were still attached like beads on a necklace.

Emma couldn't explain what was happening in Japanese, but she knew exactly why the ice had stuck to the string. She knew that saltwater froze at a lower temperature than normal water. Adding salt made the ice melt and absorb the heat in the process. When the area around it cooled, the water molecules froze and the string became stuck to them.

Emma had wondered how she'd adapt to the Japanese school but now she had maths and science classes to look forward to … and they were way more complex and interesting than her classes at home.

Sensei always showed them how to do an experiment and then they got to try it for themselves. One of Emma's favourites was making carbon dioxide and using it to blow up a balloon. Emma learned how carbon dioxide could even be used to blow out a candle.

The other thing Emma loved about her Japanese school were the lunches – big bottles of milk, Japanese curry and rice.

Her Japanese language skills were improving every day, but she always appreciated it when one of the other students slowed down and tried to help her communicate in this new language.

The curriculum was far more advanced than she was used to, so it challenged and engaged her in a way that was exciting. It made her love maths and science even more.

They were all starting to get used to this new life, but after seven months, Dad's university project finished and their time in Tokyo came to an end. But they weren't finished with Japan. Dad had a new contract in Ishinomaki, a port city near the Kitakami Mountains. Emma was excited to be back near the sea and couldn't wait to swim and try out her snorkelling equipment in the Japanese waters.

For the last part of their stay in Japan, Mum homeschooled them which was fine with Emma too. In the morning they did lessons for three hours and worked through their textbooks, and in the afternoon they were free to swim and play with the local children.

They went on a community hike over the Kitakami mountains which were lush and green and peaceful – so different from the busy streets of

Tokyo. They passed a herd of deer grazing on the slopes. The deer watched them pass, eyes round, antlers erect, and legs poised ready for flight, but the deer didn't run. The path wound around the mountains, taking them through some dense forest.

By the time they finished, they were hot and tired and ready for a swim at the beach. They plucked oysters and fresh sea urchins from the rock pools and swam and floated in the cool waters.

Ben, who liked to play jokes, picked up a sea urchin and threw it to Sam, calling out, 'Hey, catch'.

Sam was on an inflatable tube. If he let the sea urchin fall, the spikes would puncture it, so his automatic reflex was to catch the urchin. He screamed and dropped it, but it was too late – his hand was full of spines.

'That was stupid, Ben,' exclaimed Mum as she rushed over.

Emma thought Ben would be in real trouble, but Mum was too focused on trying to pick the spines out of Sam's hand. It was a bad end to a great day.

But it didn't stop them from continuing to enjoy the Japanese coastline every day until it was time to head back to Australia. Despite the language difficulties, Emma had loved her time in Japan. She had discovered that the subjects she loved most were universal and that there was a place for scientists and mathematicians anywhere in the world.

7

Underwater world

Emma was glad to be back in her beachside home, but Simon the budgie wasn't as pleased to see her as she'd expected. He had thrived at Emma's grandparents, enjoying a daily diet of freshly picked grass and Grandpa's special treats.

Emma couldn't wait to have him on her shoulder again, riding around like a pirate's parrot. But a year was a long time in the life of a bird and he didn't seem to recognise her or the rest of her family.

When Emma picked him up, Simon pecked her finger.

'Ouch!' Emma shook her finger. She spoke softly to him. 'It's me, Emma. I'm not going to hurt you.'

He pecked her again.

She tried several times, but soon realised that he didn't know her anymore and didn't seem to want to. The more they tried to befriend him, the more aggressive he became. He seemed to see them all as the enemy, trying to take him from his happy home.

'We might have to leave him with Grandma and Grandpa,' Mum suggested.

'I'm sorry. We didn't want this to happen, but he thinks this is his home now,' said Grandpa.

Reluctantly, Emma and her brothers agreed to leave Simon where he seemed to be happiest.

At home, they couldn't wait to go to the beach, slip on their snorkelling gear and plunge into the sea. Emma was happy to be back. Gliding through the deep blue water, the only sound she could hear was her breath resounding through her snorkel. A wave rolled in and buffeted her about, splashing water into the tube. Lifting her head above the surface, she expelled the water in two powerful practised blasts. Ben did the same, dropping back into the water first, with Emma following. As they swam towards her favourite place in the whole world, Crystal Pools, she could feel the waves frothing at her sides.

They hadn't been here for 12 months, but they still knew exactly where to dive. Emma kicked slowly and powerfully after Ben, keeping her fins submerged and her body horizontal so she didn't splash and scare the fish or stir up sediment and cloud the view. Ben nudged her and pointed to a giant stingray gliding past like an underwater kite. Emma froze. She was mesmerised by the stingray's grace, but she knew that the sharp barb at the base of its tail was like a hunting arrow. **Stingrays** were something to be wary of.

Stingrays in Port Phillip Bay can be 2.5 metres in diameter and up to 4.3 metres long including their tails, and weigh 350 kg.

A school of fish swam past, their scales shimmering silver in the sunlight that flicked its fingers into the water. Emma kept as still as possible so she could get a better look at the marine life around her. The water was crystal clear and some days, like today the shafts of sunlight that speared down through the water made everything sparkle. It was like a palace under the sea. She glided over reefs that were bright with pink encrusting coraline seaweed. Big bunches of mussels clung to the rocks and bright green sea lettuce shimmered in the slight currents. This beautiful, living thing was a jewel of the sea.

Next day, Emma and her brothers took butter knives from the cutlery drawer in the kitchen and went to explore the rock pools. They hopped from one smooth rock to another, stopping to peer into the water, looking for sea creatures like anemones and sea stars. Emma loved the fact that no two rock pools were the same, and each one was teaming with life. They snorkelled out to the deeper water, and using their knives, they duck-dived down to scrape **abalone** from the rocks. They needed the knives because each abalone had a large muscular foot to hold them to the rocks. The children had to be extremely quick or the abalone would sense them coming and would fix themselves so tightly to the rock that they wouldn't be able to dislodge them. Emma and her brothers were careful to only take the larger abalone home to eat.

They removed the slimy creatures from their shells and scrubbed them before slicing them thinly, then quickly frying them with lemon juice and soy sauce.

'These are the best,' declared Ben.

Emma nodded. This had to be one of her favourite treats.

She sat back in her dining chair, and closed her eyes, allowing the sea breeze from the open window to float across her face. The ocean was full of beauty and amazing marine life, and she felt so lucky to be living here.

8

Time for change

Although Emma was happy to be back with her friends, she missed the school in Tokyo, especially the amazing science experiments and the way that the science and maths had challenged her there.

Back in Australia, she had just started high school and felt that she wasn't learning many new things.

'School's boring,' she complained to her mum.

'It's only early in the year. I'm sure it'll get harder,' Mum said.

Emma frowned. 'It's not just that. I don't think our teacher believes that girls should be doing maths.

'What do you mean?'

Mum looked up from her painting and set her brushes down. After being forced out of her science career when Sam was born, Mum didn't want this happening to her daughter. She constantly encouraged Emma in her love of maths and science, saying she had just as much right to choose science for her career as any man.

'It's true!' Emma put her hands on her hips. 'When a girl puts up her hand to ask a question, our teacher ignores it. When a boy puts up his hand, the question gets answered straight away, even if it's a stupid one.'

'That doesn't sound fair,' said Mum.

'It's not!'

'So what happens when you want to ask something?' Mum covered the painting, picked up her brushes and stood up.

Emma shrugged. 'I never have questions. The teacher always gives me problems that I know how to do. But I want to know why he thinks girls shouldn't do maths.'

'Maybe you should ask him,' said Mum.

Next maths class, Emma had her hand up for more than five minutes, but the teacher kept sailing past as if she wasn't there. She thought about calling out, but she didn't want to be rude, and she was was sure that Mr Harvey had seen her. It made her angry, but it also made her determined that she would show him that a girl could do maths just as well as any boy – and this girl, maybe even better.

She started helping the other girls with their maths. At least it made classes more interesting. At home, maths and science had always been part of Emma's everyday life. Mum and Dad were constantly explaining how things worked. If Emma wanted to know why the ocean had waves or the sunlight in the rockpools was dappled, or why the sky was blue, they explained it to her. She was a sponge for knowledge, wanting to find out as much as she could about the world around her.

But at school, she constantly came up against walls, walls that seemed to have been built to keep girls out. It wasn't just the maths teacher who wouldn't help the girls. The English teacher also refused to ask girls questions. He never picked Emma, even when she had her hand up the longest and knew the answer. He only read out stories about adventurous boys, and the boys always seemed to get the highest marks.

At least the science teacher didn't care who you were as long as you loved his subject as much as he did. And he appreciated Emma's enthusiasm.

When the science teacher asked, 'Does anyone know why clothes dry faster in a breeze?' Emma was the first to put up her hand.

'Emma, let's hear from you,' he said.

'The breeze causes faster evaporation because it constantly brings new dry air next to the clothes and the air sucks the water from the clothes and that causes them to dry quicker.'

Emma didn't even know how she knew the answers sometimes, but science was always such a big and exciting topic of discussion at home.

Science was clearly a possible career path for Emma, but there were so many things she loved and was good at. She played piano and flute and she was also a great communicator. The time she had spent in France and Japan where she barely spoke the language at first had taught her to be an observer, picking up information from what people said with their eyes, not just their mouths and their actions. It also gave her empathy for people in situations where the language wasn't familiar to them. She understood their sense of isolation, what it was like to be left out.

So, when Rotary exchange student, Mara, arrived at the school from Germany with only basic English skills, Emma happily became her translator. She was able to break down what was being said so that Mara could better understand and use facial expressions and gestures to convey meaning.

Although she did lots of activities outside class, like playing in the school orchestra and singing in the choir, she was becoming increasingly annoyed with the differences between how boys and girls were treated by some teachers. Emma had been raised with the belief that she could do anything her brothers could, and she couldn't understand why that wasn't supported in the world outside her family.

One day, she came home from school frustrated and determined to do something about it.

'It happened again in English today,' she told her parents at the dinner table. 'I had my hand up and

Mr Baker turned his back on me and asked Tom, who was sitting on the other side of the room!'

'Maybe he didn't see that your hand was up,' suggested Ben.

Emma shook her head. 'He stared straight at me before he turned his head.'

'What do you want us to do? We can speak to him if you like,' said Mum.

Emma shook her head. 'It won't do any good. He'll probably just ignore me more.' Emma had made up her mind. 'I want to go to a different school.'

Dad nodded. 'I don't blame you.'

'Maybe it's for the best,' said Mum. 'You haven't been challenged there for a long time.'

'I've heard good things about MacRobertson Girl's High,' said Dad. 'It's not far from here.'

Emma liked the thought of an all-girls' school. Teachers there couldn't discriminate against her just because she was a girl.

She filled out the application form and a few weeks later, a letter arrived inviting her to sit the scholarship test. Emma breezed through it and was soon offered a place. She would be sorry to leave her friends behind, but she was looking forward to a fresh start. Emma couldn't wait for the Open Day for new students and the chance to find out everything she could about her new school.

Dressed in her sneakers, jeans and white tee, she hopped on the train that would take her to Melbourne and then the tram to MacRob High. She was welcomed to the school by Penny, a student not much older than her. Penny was immaculately dressed and very friendly, but as she showed her around the school, Emma's heart sank. MacRob clearly had a lot of rules, just like the school she was at now. Emma started to wonder if this was the place for her.

She wanted a school where she could learn new things, but she also wanted somewhere that encouraged her to think and speak freely.

9

A chance meeting

That afternoon, Emma caught the bus home from MacRob High. She stared out the window, deep in thought, mulling over everything she had seen and heard at the Open Day.

'Emma?' A familiar voice called her name, and she spun around.

'I thought it was you,' said Nandi. She used to be at Emma's school, and they had been in choir and orchestra together, but Nandi had left last year.

Emma had always admired the older girl. Nandi wasn't in school uniform but she had a backpack on her shoulder. 'Hi Nandi, how are you?' She smiled.

'I'm great!' Nandi swung into the seat beside her. 'Where've you been?'

'Checking out my new school – MacRob High.' Emma frowned.

'What's the matter? You don't look too impressed by it?'

'They had great facilities, especially for someone like me who loves science, but there were a lot of rules.'

Nandi laughed. 'You should come to my school. Things are way more casual … and it's so awesome. I bet the facilities at Uni High are just as good as MacRob. Seriously, I love it. You should check it out.'

Nandi did seem happy, and Emma certainly had doubts about the new school she had chosen for herself.

'Casual clothes day?' She asked.

Nandi shook her head. 'No uniform. That's one of the things I like about it. They encourage you to be an individual.'

Emma really liked the sound of University High, but her mind was racing. When she was accepted into MacRob, her parents had been so proud. She didn't want to disappoint them. But instinct told her it wasn't the school for her.

'That sounds perfect.' Emma sighed.

Nandi nodded. 'And the only expectations you have to conform to are the ones you have for yourself.'

Nandi wrote the school's phone number on a piece of paper and handed it to her friend. 'You should at least ring them. You could probably get a music scholarship. I remember how great you were in the orchestra.'

Emma was filled with a mix of excitement and dread. She wasn't sure what to do. If she told her parents that she wanted to go to University High instead of MacRob, they'd think that she was being easily led by Nandi. It wasn't that at all. She'd had doubts about MacRob as soon as she'd walked around the school. Apart from the lack of boys, it didn't seem much different from the school she was leaving. Uni High on the other hand sounded like a polar opposite, in a good way.

But there was no point in bothering her parents with her desire to go to Uni High, when she might not even get in.

Mum was out shopping when Emma got home, so before she changed her mind, Emma picked up the phone and rang the number that Nandi had given her. She spoke to the bursar who seemed impressed by her initiative and invited her to sit for the scholarship test in a few Saturdays' time and said she could fill out the forms on the day.

*

The morning of the test, Emma rose early and had a quick swim at the beach to calm herself. Then she showered, dressed and set off for the train before anyone was up, leaving a note to say she had gone to the city and would be back in the afternoon.

The testing process was very different from MacRob's. For University High, she only had to do a music audition playing the flute and give them a copy of her results from school.

Afterwards, she felt great. She liked the vibe of the school. It seemed to be run more like a university than a high school, with students being encouraged

to be independent. Following the tests, she met up with Holly for lunch. Emma was ravenous; she had been too nervous to eat breakfast.

When she got home, she told her parents all about where she and Holly had been, but not about the real reason she'd gone to the city. Although she felt guilty for not telling them, she couldn't see the point in worrying them about something that might never happen.

Waiting for a letter from the school was the hard bit now, so she tried to put it out of her mind.

Several weeks went by then one afternoon, Mum came into Emma's room while she was doing her homework and dropped an envelope on her desk. It was addressed to Emma and had the University High School crest in the left-hand corner.

Emma's fingers shook as she opened it. She had waited so long for this, but she could hardly bring herself to look at what was inside. When she finally read the letter, she broke into a huge grin.

'What is it?' said Mum.

'I got in! I got a place at University High!'

Mum's eyebrows went up. 'University High? But what about MacRob?'

The words poured out of Emma. 'I'm sorry I didn't say anything, but I wasn't sure I'd get in and I didn't want to worry you.'

Mum smiled. 'I'm not worried, just surprised. What happened?'

'When I went to MacRob's Open Day, I realised it probably wasn't the school for me. Too many rules.' Emma grinned.

Mum laughed. 'So why University High?'

'On the way home from the Open Day, I met Nandi – you remember her, she used to be in the school band with me. She left last year. She goes to Uni High and loves it. They don't have a uniform and they encourage you to think freely. And when I went there and spoke to them on the day of the tests, I really liked it.'

'I thought you had to live nearby to go there,' said Mum.

'You do. But I got a music scholarship.' Emma was still a bit nervous, wondering how her parents would take this news.

But Mum hugged her. 'You're old enough to make your own decisions – and it does sound like a good school for you. I'm really proud that you did all this off your own bat.'

Emma felt the stress lift. 'Thanks, Mum. I can't go yet because the scholarship is for Year 10, 11 and 12, but I'm happy to wait.'

Mum smiled. 'If you're going to be a scientist, patience is definitely a virtue.'

Emma grinned. 'I haven't decided what I'm going to do yet.'

10

Young activist

Emma loved her new school right from the start. She loved the fact that there was no uniform, the freedom of not being forced to wear skirts or dresses that hampered her physical and mental freedom and labelled her as a 'girl' rather than a student. Wearing a school uniform had made her feel like she was part of a herd, conforming to school rules she didn't agree with. Now she could be an individual, wearing what she liked and not having to worry about uniform infringements.

And, it offered so many subject choices and extracurricular opportunities. Emma took advantage of as many as she could, joining the senior band, the orchestra, the senior choir and ensemble. This meant spending many of her lunchtimes and long hours after school immersed in music. This was Emma's kind of school.

At the time, the government was running a program called, 'Girls do the maths', to encourage girls to study maths and science. Emma didn't need encouragement. These were her favourite subjects. So, she was shocked to discover when she arrived at University High, that in spite of the government campaign and the free-thinking attitudes of the school, hardly any girls were taking these subjects.

At her old school, girls she knew in Year 9 were already talking about opting out of maths and science when they could in Year 11 because they didn't think that they were smart enough. Emma had argued with her friend, Holly, 'Of course you're smart enough. Nobody says you have to be top of the class. Boys are encouraged to do maths and science whether they're smart or not. Why can't girls be the same?'

But Holly wouldn't be persuaded, and neither would many of the other girls in Emma's year level, even ones who'd had a lot of academic success. And teachers didn't try to talk them into doing maths and science like they did with the boys.

Emma couldn't believe that the same thing was happening at University High – girls didn't take maths and science classes because they didn't think they were smart enough. Boys didn't care if they were smart or not. They didn't have to. They picked and were welcomed into these classes regardless of their abilities. Emma was shocked to discover that only three girls were doing physics in her entire Year 11 and 12 classes.

Gender equality wasn't the only thing on Emma's mind. She was also worried about the environment and thought that people could be doing more for the planet. She remembered back to the dust storm in Grade Four when she'd learned that farm chemicals were leaching into waterways and killing the animal and plant life that lived there. Human pollution was damaging the natural world.

If Emma saw something wrong, she tried to fix it, so the lack of recycling at University High was something that had caught her attention straightaway.

'Why don't we recycle paper and tin and plastics?' She asked her Year Level Coordinator.

'Nobody has really thought about it, I suppose, or if they have, they haven't taken action,' said Mr Stanley.

'They should have.' Emma held up a handful of rubbish from the playground. 'We can't just let all this go to **landfill**.'

Mr Stanley nodded. 'So what do you propose to do?'

'Make it happen.'

Landfill

A place where waste is crushed into small pieces and buried. Without oxygen, it causes a dangerous greenhouse gas called methane to be created. It contributes to global warming.

Emma formed a student group and successfully advocated for a recycling system at the school. It was 1989 and for the first time in its history, University High students and staff worked out a plan to dispose of their rubbish in an environmentally responsible way. This meant having separate bins for different types of rubbish so that tins, plastic and paper were not sent to landfill. This was incredibly radical at the time as in 1989 only 3% of local councils in Australia were doing any recycling.

In 2018, 15-year-old **Greta Thunberg** refused to go to school and went on strike outside the Swedish Parliament to try and get adults to do something about climate change. Soon school children in more than 120 countries around the world, including Australia, joined Greta on a global climate strike.

The students striking in Australia had 3 demands for the government:

1. Say 'no' to all fossil fuels.
2. Power Australia with 100% renewables by 2050.
3. Stop the Adani coalmine in Queensland.

Emma and her schoolmates were setting an inspiring example of how school students could have a great idea to improve something and, with their teachers' support, inspire other schools and councils and even governments, to follow suit.

In Year 10, Emma had abandoned previous ideas of becoming a teacher, doctor or a psychiatrist, deciding instead to be a science journalist.

It seemed like the perfect career for her – combining her talents of science and communication.

Her work experience during that year was at *The Australian* newspaper, which she found disappointing. A journalist's life was clearly far from glamorous. She wasn't assigned any stories of her own, but instead spent the week trailing after *The Australian* journalists and looking on as they researched and wrote their articles.

She was surprised by how shallow their stories were, too. They seemed to just skim the surface of the topic they were writing about whereas she had expected them to delve deeper, to find out more, to strive for truth and justice in their stories.

Perhaps she needed to rethink her career choice. Maybe journalism was not for her? She loved the idea of writing articles, though, and soon took on the role of editor of *Ubique*, the University High school newspaper that came out twice a year. Emma used *Ubique* to encourage students to express themselves, to write articles about things that mattered to them. Sometimes she didn't have enough content for the paper so she asked her friends to write a piece.

When a friend wrote a quite controversial article, Emma gave it a double-page spread because she thought it was such an important topic. She felt it would be enlightening for the school community and allow students to walk in the shoes of people with diverse backgrounds and lives. This was pretty radical for a student paper at the time.

It was welcomed by the students, but many parents didn't appreciate *this* kind of free expression, which didn't worry Emma. She refused to remove the article because she believed that every student should be able to contribute their point of view to the school newspaper and share their experiences.

In spite of her disappointing experiences at *The Australian* and the backlash from printing the article, Emma continued as editor of *Ubique*, more committed than ever to giving her fellow students a public space to have their say. Between her studies, editing the newspaper, her music and her friends, Emma didn't have time for much else these days, even the beach.

Each issue of *Ubique* was set out in the final format just over the road at the office of the Melbourne University student newspaper so Emma soon made some great contacts there. She began to think of the university as a potential next step in her education. It had a great reputation for science studies and science journalism was still her career of choice, combining the two things she loved most.

She knew she'd need good marks, and her Year 12 was going to be a huge workload because she had gained entry to University High with a music scholarship. So, on top of her five science, maths and English subjects, she had to take music theory and music practice.

Sometimes her eyeballs hurt from so much study, and she practised flute so much, that her fingers and head ached. Although she had a lot to get through, it taught her how to manage her time better – a skill that would be really useful for everything she was going to do in the future. It was still exhausting, though, and she couldn't wait for the end of the school year when her studies would be over and she could spend time travelling and doing the other things she loved.

On her final day of school, she felt sad about walking through the school gates for the last time.

But she was also excited about what lay ahead, and excited about going to Melbourne University, providing she got the marks she needed. Her goal spurred her on to work even harder – exams were only a couple of weeks away.

When it came time to sit her exams alongside thousands of other Year 12 students, she was more nervous than she'd ever been. Even though she'd studied hard, there was so much at stake.

The day finally arrived for the first exam – English. The students were milling outside the hall, noisily talking about what they thought might be in the exams. She tried not to listen. If she hadn't studied it by now, it was too late.

After each exam, she hurried home to do last-minute study for the next one – she didn't want to stay for the post-mortem afterwards either.

*

During high school, Emma had earned money teaching flute to young children, so after she finished her exams, she used her savings to travel around Indonesia and Europe by herself, all the while trying not to think about her results. She had tried her hardest at school, and that was the best she could do. When the results finally came in January, she was far away in the Netherlands so they had to be phoned through.

'Congratulations, Emma! You've done very well,' said Mum. 'We're so proud of you!'

Emma couldn't stop smiling. She had graduated with outstanding marks and so had the other two girls in her Physics class. Between them, they'd achieved the top three Physics results in the school. Emma would like to have visited her teachers from her first high school to show them just what girls could do.

Her Year 12 marks opened up a world of opportunities. Mum and Dad were full of ideas about where to next.

'You could study Law,' said Dad.

'Or Medicine,' said Mum.

'That's not what I want, though,' Emma said.

'But you're smart, you have empathy and great communication skills. You'd be a fantastic doctor,' said Dad.

In the early years of high school, Emma had thought about being a doctor, but now she was determined to be a science journalist.

'I want to inspire girls to love science as much as I do,' she said.

'That's a pretty great goal,' said Mum.

'Science is so amazing,' said Emma. 'I want to help people understand just how awesome it is. If people have a better understanding of the world they live in, they'll be more likely to look after it. I can make this happen as a science journalist, but not as a doctor.'

'Fair enough,' said Dad. 'You have to do what makes you happy, what calls to you.'

Emma knew exactly what she wanted to do.

'I'm going to enrol in a science degree at Melbourne Uni and then after I finish that, I'll do a journalism internship.'

'Sounds like you have it all worked out,' said Mum.

11

Sink or swim

Emma was in her element at university. She loved the old buildings surrounded by beautiful tall trees, the quadrangles, the great **Baillieu Library** with its millions of books and journals to explore, and the buzz of thousands of students in one place.

While many first-year students got lost on the huge campus, Emma was completely familiar with

> The **Baillieu Library** has 3.5 million items (books, DVDs, photos, music scores, journals). Each year, there are 3 million visitors to it and 42 million loan transactions from it.

it, having spent so much time there when she was still at school. She was awed to think that so many great Australian leaders from politicians to scientists and educators, business people to philanthropists, had walked these paths since the university was founded in 1853. She couldn't wait to learn and to grasp every opportunity with both hands.

Biology: the study of life and living things that have at least one cell.

Cells: the building blocks of all living things.

The year started well. She made new friends easily and had her first introduction to **Biology**, a subject that she hadn't been able to fit into her busy schedule at school but loved, right from the start.

She was fascinated to learn how living things interacted with each other and with the environment in which they live. Just as humans relied on the natural world for survival – food, shelter and to reproduce for their species to continue – the same was true for all other living things. It was something she hadn't thought about much before. She had just taken for granted that these things were there when you needed them.

It made her look deeper into the marine environment she loved so much which was when she realised how things had changed in just two generations. When her grandfather was young, he had hunted for food during the **Great Depression** in that part of Port Phillip Bay where she had grown up. Now it was no longer abundant with fish.

The industrial area near her home had grown and she could now smell chemicals in the air. She wondered if that was leading to the dwindling wildlife in the ocean.

And more and more household rubbish seemed to be finding its way onto the beaches and into the bay. One day Emma found a cormorant with plastic caught around its legs and beak. Although they took it straight to the vet, it couldn't be saved.

People didn't seem to realise how much damage they were doing to the environment by their careless actions, by dumping rubbish and polluting the land and waterways with chemicals. She began to read more and more scientific papers on the topic. Why wasn't it being splashed all over the newspapers? Were the big businesses that operated the industrial plants near her home so powerful that they could get away with damaging the environment without the government stopping them or the media talking about it?

Did journalists really have the freedom to report the truth? Was science a valued profession? As a science journalist would she be able to truly help the world around her? As editor of *Ubique*, people had tried to censor her work. They didn't seem to want to read anything that they found confronting.

That's when Emma decided that maybe science journalism wasn't the career for her, after all. So, what should she do with her life? For the first time since primary school, she had no career goal, nothing to aim for. What was the point in her spending years at university if there was no great and useful career at the end of it?

Normally a bubbly and confident person, this realisation left her feeling flat and let down. She had worked so hard to get here, but now there was nothing to motivate and inspire her to keep going. Now she could understand how some of her friends felt, who had never had any idea what they wanted to do with their lives. They had admired her drive and the fact that she had a life plan. All that was gone.

Emma forged on with her degree, hoping that her mojo would return, that she would find something to inspire her. She decided to choose subjects that were interesting in their own right. She followed her passions, attended lectures and tutorials, completed her assigned homework and sat her exams, desperately hoping that she might find her destiny along the way, not realising that she already had.

She also immersed herself in extra-curricular activities in the same way she had at high school, joining student groups and getting involved with causes. Motivated by science and environmental issues, and being a strong advocate for people's rights, she ended up being voted President of the Student Union at the university. In this role she created brand-new student leadership positions for the Environment and for Student Welfare Services. At last she felt as if she was doing something worthwhile at uni even if her studies were not going to her original plan.

But as she worked her way through her degree, she became more and more interested in biology, particularly the way human activities impacted on the environment. It was something she'd thought about a lot since the huge dust storm of her childhood. She also became fascinated with the reasons why humans interacted with the natural world in the way they did. Why some people were happy just to swim and explore the ocean's depths and others used it for water sports and even a dumping ground for household and chemical waste.

Ecological research became her new passion. It combined all the things she was good at and loved: her science, journalism, environmental and public advocacy interests.

Philosophy of science asks questions such as what is science, how reliable are scientific theories, what is the purpose of science.

At last, her enthusiasm and energy were back. With a new plan for her career and new inspiration, Emma returned to being her bubbly, confidant self. She decided to do extra studies into ecology and the **philosophy of science** to give her a deeper understanding of the natural world and how we study it.

Emma felt she had more purpose as she entered the final year of her degree, but now she had other questions about becoming a university lecturer. Why did female lecturers only seem to work in biology and not subjects like physics, chemistry or maths? Was her career going to be limited in the same way her early schooling had been, just because she was a woman?

It seemed that gender equality was still far from reality. Not much had changed since her mother had been forced to abandon her career as a chemist and become a painter because she wanted to spend more time with her children. But Emma had found a career that combined her love of science and love of the ocean. There was no way she was going to let anything hold her back, especially **discrimination**.

Emma was also determined to get to where the action was, to do field research, to make important discoveries, to make a difference. Surely there must be other women who had taken this career path? She started looking for role models, for women who had proved that anything was possible in the world of science, regardless of gender. Sure, there was the remarkable **Marie Curie** who won two Nobel Prizes for her research into radioactivity, and **Rachel Carson**, a science-trained journalist who wrote the influential book *Silent Spring* that woke up the world to the environmental impact of agricultural chemicals. But Emma was looking for a living mentor.

Completing her degree with another impressive set of results, Emma prepared to begin further studies. She was grateful for the support of her family in her decision – her parents had understood and accepted that she wasn't going to be a medical doctor or a lawyer.

'Be the scientist you want to be,' they said.

But Emma's grandparents weren't as understanding. Her grandma on her father's side greeted the news that she was going to do her **PhD** with, 'Surely you have enough degrees by now. Isn't it time to settle down and have children?'

Emma sighed. So much had changed, but so much hadn't changed. Why couldn't she have both – a partner, children *and* a career? Men did it all the time, so why couldn't women?

12

Dr Emma

For her PhD, Emma decided to research the waters around her home. She wanted to find out more about the plant life, animals and **microbes** that lived there.

> **Microbes**
>
> Living things that are so small you can't see them without a microscope. Microbes include things like bacteria, viruses, algae and fungi.

She had seen the growing pollution of the area and she wanted to understand if the activities of the factories and manufacturing plants were damaging the environment. She focused her research on the effects of copper pollution on the marine life at Breakwater Pier in Port Phillip Bay.

As if she weren't busy enough with her PhD research, she became newsletter editor of the *Marine Scientists Bulletin* which came out four times a year. Marine scientists often worked in remote locations, so they eagerly looked forward to the Bulletin to discover what their colleagues were researching and discovering around Australia.

The editor's role was a great way for Emma to network with colleagues all over Australia and find out what was happening in the world of Marine Science. Emma was also on the National Council of the Australian Marine Sciences Association.

In 2002 she completed her doctorate. As part of her studies, she had conducted research in Port Phillip Bay to find out what effect increased copper levels would have on a marine environment. She had used treated plaster blocks to create localised concentrations of copper that were much higher than the levels in the surrounding environment. Her goal was to measure the effects of very short bursts of pollution on marine life. These sorts of experiments had not been done before, and the outcome could have very big consequences.

After collecting and analysing all the data, her research showed that significant levels of copper led to a large reduction in the sea squirt population and that barnacle numbers were reduced by up to one third.

Emma had shown that pollution events that might occur during spills could have a serious negative impact on the environment. She had also discovered that pollution of oceans and rivers and other waterways leading into them, weakened the local marine communities. This made them vulnerable to invasion by non-native species like the vase sea squirt or the brown lace coral.

Now that she'd completed her studies, Emma started to look for a job in her chosen field. There were so many ways she could apply her skills and knowledge to because marine biologists could work anywhere in the world. But Emma was now married and knew she couldn't leave her home country just yet because her husband's work opportunities were in Australia. Luckily, there were plenty of jobs

in coastal management, reef ecology, invertebrate diversity, fisheries and marine pollution here anyway. In fact, there were too many choices!

'I don't know which way to go,' she said to her family.

'What do you love doing most?' asked her husband.

'There are so many things. I love science and communication. I love research, working with people, collecting data; and I also like teaching. You can see my dilemma,' she shrugged.

'So why don't you look for a job that has all those things?' he suggested.

Emma was determined to find a job that would fit in with her lifestyle and family. Where she couldn't be forced out when she decided to have children. She knew that if she intended to build a career, she would have to make her mark in the field of marine biology before she had a family. She was looking for a lot in one job. And even if she found such a position, there was no guarantee that she'd get it.

Soon after, Emma saw an advertisement for an Associate Lecturer in the Department of Biological,

Earth and Environmental Sciences at the University of New South Wales.

The job sounded perfect – a combination of her science and communication skills and a workplace aligned with her interest in learning and the environment. But the university was in Sydney, so she and her husband would have to leave their families and friends and the place where they grew up.

The University of New South Wales wasn't Oxford or Cambridge or some of the famous international workplaces where her marine biologist friends were hoping to find employment, but this position was a full-time permanent job. And there could be research opportunities to help her advance her career. She decided to apply.

The interview and selection process was rigorous and intense. Emma had to fly up to Sydney and sit before a panel of five interviewers at the university and explain why she was the best person for the job and why she wanted it. The competition was tough and a woman was less likely to be chosen. She just hoped she'd made a good impression.

A few days later when she got the phone call letting her know that she was successful, it was a bittersweet moment sharing the news with friends and family. Emma was elated with her good fortune, landing her dream job almost straight after finishing her doctorate. But she would leaving Melbourne. On the upside, it was only a short flight between the two cities, and she had no doubt she and her husband would have a lot of visitors!

Dr Emma Johnston was about to take the first step into the diverse and exciting world of marine science. Her job was located near Sydney Harbour – an exciting new aquatic playground for her to explore.

13

Underwater office

After spending all that time at university with very few female role models, Emma hoped to find them in the workplace. She wanted to meet other women who were passionate about their careers, who shared her ambition to protect the environment from damage by humans. She was desperate to know that equal opportunity was possible in her chosen field.

So she was disappointed to discover that only one other woman worked in a department of 30 male academics, and she retired when Emma had been in the job just a year.

Right at the outset, Emma was different from some of the other members of her department in many ways. She worried about the physical and mental welfare of her students as well as their academic success. She provided them with pastoral care, despite the fact that she was sometimes told by male colleagues, 'not to get involved'.

She took great pride in the quality of her teaching. Sometimes it took a whole week to develop one new practical class for her students because she wanted it to be cutting edge and easy to access. She wanted to make their education more engaging than hers had been.

Emma wanted a female mentor who knew what it was like to work in a male-dominated environment, who appreciated her skills and intelligence and understood how important it was for her to be treated equally. She needed someone who empowered her to trust her instincts and drive projects, and who would encourage her to take risks and step out of her comfort zone.

But she soon found that there were no women who could take on this role so she found male mentors instead. They showed her the way and checked in on her progress.

So Emma made up her mind that when she was established in her career, she would be that role model and mentor to other girls and women, just as her mother had always been such an amazing source of support and encouragement to her. She would try to be visible and outgoing so that more junior staff and students could see a female enjoying her job and feel comfortable about coming to her for help or advice. She would do this even when she wasn't feeling confident herself.

> Although Emma worked hard to change things and since 2016 at the University of NSW, the percentage of women in senior roles has risen from 17% to 27% – that's still not even one third of the total positions.

In spite of the difficulties of floundering in an environment that wasn't supportive of women, Emma refused to give up. She was passionate about this career path and knew that other women would be too if they were given the opportunity.

Especially at senior levels where important decisions are made that can bring about changes.

The job itself was rewarding and varied. As an associate lecturer, she prepared classes, gave lectures, marked work, and encouraged personal development in her students. She did this for five subjects a year plus she organised programs and field trips. It was hectic. On top of that, she had to find time for research.

Sydney Harbour was the ideal research destination. With a shoreline stretching over 240 kilometres, it encompassed 54 kilometres of waterways. She was surprised to find that in spite of the impact of thousands of people working and living and playing there, the waters were abundant with a great diversity of marine life.

Attempts had been made to keep the harbour clean since the early 1900s when rat catchers used to trap infected rats to try and stop the spread of **bubonic plague**. In the 1930s, rubbish collectors would use rowing boats to collect rubbish and dead animals floating in the harbour. It wasn't until the 1950s that the boats were given engines!

After the Maritime Authority recognised the environmental significance of Sydney Harbour, it made a commitment to take action to improve and preserve it.

But as Emma discovered, there was still a great deal of work needed because the marine life in the harbour was constantly being exposed to pollution from households, businesses and tourists. Rubbish and fuel from boats and ships would spill into the harbour and visiting cargo ships would accidentally bring in foreign species of marine animals attached to their bows.

There was another danger on the horizon that would affect the whole planet – **climate change**. Sea levels were already on the rise in the harbour, causing erosion, and Emma knew that warmer water would have a significant impact on the local marine life. So that became an important part of her research focus. When Emma started teaching

Climate Change

Long-term changes in climate and temperature that can cause damage to the environment and extreme weather events like massive storms, floods, extensive and fierce bushfires. Using fossil fuels like petrol, coal and gas is a major cause of climate change.

in 2001, although climate change was part of the curriculum and evidence of the danger to the planet was clear and growing, nobody seemed to be paying much attention to it.

Over the summer breaks there were no classes at the university, which was, Emma's only time for research in her 'office' under the sea in Sydney Harbour, swimming through sea grass meadows and kelp forests, and gliding over coral reefs. She used an underwater notepad, collected samples and took photos to gather vital information about the underwater world.

She wanted to know more and she wanted to share that knowledge with others, believing that if people knew and understood the need for change, they would be more willing to embrace it, for the good of the planet. So for Emma, research was like stepping over the edge into the unknown, and she was excited by the thought of major ecological discoveries that could be just around the corner.

14

Understanding Sydney Harbour

Although she was raised on Port Phillip Bay in Melbourne, Emma had grown to love Sydney and had developed a special connection to the harbour. When she looked out over the water she imagined how it must have been in times gone by when Southern Right Whales used the harbour as a safe haven from storms, and seals sprawled on the rocks sunning themselves.

There are more than 500 species of fish in the harbour, twice the number recorded for the whole coastline of the United Kingdom. And Emma had discovered almost every type of ocean habitat.

But the marine life was still feeling the effects of pollution.

Emma combined data collected in Sydney Harbour and many other NSW estuaries with laboratory studies of pollution and found that the pollution of waterways, particularly by copper from manufacturing, helped foreign species flourish and take over habitats by competing with local species and forcing them out. She identified that cargo ships combined with pollution had caused a huge problem for this beautiful harbour.

Out of more than 300 introduced species now competing with local marine life, two thirds had arrived attached to yacht or ship hulls.

In 2012, she was appointed the first Director of the Sydney Harbour Research Program at the Sydney Institute of Marine Science. One of her projects was to bring together 35 research scientists from around Sydney to help identify how they could best understand and assist the marine life in Sydney Harbour by discovering what habitats had been lost or damaged.

Emma was asked to report to the Sydney Institute of Marine Science board on the program's findings. She concluded that there needed to be more research into water quality, micro-plastics and debris as well as plankton levels

A great result of the research was the creation of the World Harbour Program to spread knowledge across the globe.

They also received funding to study how they might modify the harbour shoreline to restore the marine life.

Eco-concrete: concrete designed to have a less negative impact on the environment.

Algae: a simple, non-flowering plant found in a moist environment

Crustaceans: mostly aquatic animals with many pairs of legs, a tough outer skeleton, and a segmented body like a crab or lobster.

Molluscs: have a soft body and live in water or a damp environment and usually have an external shell like a snail or mussel.

The money was used to create experimental living sea walls using **eco-concrete** – specially designed habitats for **crustaceans, algae** and **molluscs to grow in**. And they worked!

*

Since European settlement around the Sydney Harbour, industries and humans have drained their waste into it, but the ancient, drowned valley with its three-kilometre opening to the ocean allowed it to be flushed every day with clean sea water as the tides sucked water back and forth from the ocean. Emma believes that this is what has saved the harbour from more severe pollution and why many fish have survived there.

After the sea walls were built, the seagrass, mangroves, saltbush and abundant species of fish flourished again which Emma saw as a message of hope. Neglected and damaged ecosystems could recover and become places of great environmental value as well as supporting the activities of humans living around them.

So much had been done to understand the harbour but Emma still worried that it wasn't enough, especially with climate change and micro-plastics being emerging threats.

With climate change causing rising sea levels and increased water temperatures, one solution she suggested was to eco-engineer rockpools into the foreshores and shade them as well to provide havens for marine plants and animals.

Her team's research on micro-plastics found clothing fibres all the way through from the sediments of the harbour to the stomachs of dead fish. How was that possible? To investigate whether micro-plastic fibres might be shed from fleecy jackets or other clothes made from artificial fibres every time they were washed, they built an experimental laundromat.

The team also wanted to find out the types of fabrics that would release fewer fibres, to help clothing companies make more eco-friendly clothing. Emma hopes that washing machines manufacturers will get on board and design machines to include micro-fibre filters.

15

An icy invitation

As editor of the Marine Science Association bulletin when she was doing her PhD, Emma had come into contact with many marine scientists who were doing incredible research in all parts of the Oceania region.

One day, she was in her office (not the underwater one!), marking student work when the phone rang. It was Erica, a colleague she'd met back then.

After they'd discussed what they'd been doing, Erica asked, 'How adventurous are you feeling?'

Emma was always up for a challenge.

'I'll give anything a try,' she replied.

'How about a research trip to Antarctica?'

'Antarctica? Seriously?'

Erica laughed. 'I was supposed to go, but I'm pregnant so now's not a great time for me, but I thought you'd make the perfect replacement.'

'I'd love to!' Emma said without hesitation.

'There's pretty rigorous training and preparation,' said Erica.

'I'd expect that. Antarctica's not a place where you want to take risks,' said Emma.

Antarctica is the coldest, windiest, driest continent, and contains 90% of all the ice on earth. Emma had read enough and seen enough documentaries to know that Antarctica was a harsh wilderness where temperatures were only just above freezing in summer. But the prospect was very exciting because it was home to some of the most amazing marine life. It was also a place where scientists had died in ice storms and from falling down crevasses. Emma wasn't exactly a fan of the cold, and she knew it would be dangerous, but she loved the idea of such an unexpected adventure.

So, after agreeing to go, Emma fluctuated between excitement and trepidation. It was an awesome opportunity, but even if they were careful, the expedition was still very risky. Could she withstand the extreme conditions? Was she physically and mentally strong enough to live in Antarctica for three months? On the other hand, being offered the chance to dive under the ice was the opportunity of a lifetime.

In the end, her adventurous spirit and concern for the environment soon outweighed her fears. In the 100 years or so that humans had been visiting Antarctica, they'd caused harm to the environment. Now Australian scientists wanted to undo that damage. Some species like Antarctic fur seals had been hunted almost to extinction. As well, expeditions before Emma's had taken their toll on the formerly pristine wilderness.

Human waste had been discharged into the sea, the soil had been contaminated, rubbish had been left, and **cairns** and tracks left by scientists and explorers had disturbed the fragile environment,

Cairns
Human-made piles of stones.

damaging habitats and killing marine and plant life.

Fish numbers were also being affected by overfishing and pollution.

Scientists had realised how important the clean air, water and ice of Antarctica were to help them understand how the earth was changing. By making comparisons with more densely populated areas, it helped them understand how the Earth's environment was changing naturally and because of human activity

This unique continent needed to be preserved, not just for the animals and plant life that lived there. If the Antarctic ice sheets melted, they could cause sea level rise that would not end for many centuries. Emma couldn't wait to be part of such an important project. The research itself, diving to collect specimens and data about marine life and doing laboratory-based experiments, wouldn't be much different from what she was used to. But the conditions would be the most extreme she had ever experienced.

Emma and her team were going to Antarctica for two important reasons – rubbish and research.

Antarctica is so cold that the natural processes that help get rid of waste and pollution in other parts of the world take a lot longer so there is an increased build up. Even **organic materials** that might decay quickly in other places take decades to decompose in Antarctica.

Organic materials , whether manufactured or not, come from living things, like plants and animals.

One of the goals of Emma's team was to conduct research so that the success of the clean-up could be tested. They had to find out how extensive the damage was, test if it would be reduced by the clean-up work, and identify ways to limit further pollution to the precious Antarctic environment.

They knew already that in other places a lot of damage had been done. For instance, in the Ross Sea near the American McMurdo base, scientists had found penguins, sponges, fish and marine worms with traces of chemicals in them which were probably from human wastewater. Marine litter from ships including bits of fishing nets, fishing lines, boxes and strapping had also found its way into the sea. Birds and seals that got tangled in them were injured and eventually died.

Emma's family was excited about her Antarctic adventure, but they were anxious about the dangers she would face too.

'Sounds fascinating,' her husband said.

Emma nodded. She was excited to see what it was like for marine plants and animals living in Antarctica.

'Our goal is to see whether the same processes that happen in warmer coastal waters happen down south,' she said. 'We want to see if they are more or less sensitive to the same pollutants so that we know if our protection guidelines are going to work in the frozen south. We'll be collecting all sorts of information about the breeding and feeding habits of species like sponges. And they have these amazing kelp forests there and invertebrate gardens full of anemones, and fields of **fan worms**.'

'What happens if you get sick? It's a long way from home.'

'They have a doctor stationed down there and we'll be doing extensive first aid training for when we're working remotely. Don't worry, we'll be fine,' said Emma. 'Seriously, this isn't your average first aid course. And I'm even going to the dentist beforehand to get my teeth checked.'

Although she was glad of it, Emma couldn't believe how much preparation went into the trip. All the scientists attended a briefing workshop. They were given an intensive introduction into what it would be like living and working in Antarctica. The workshop was also a great way to get to know other people who would be going on the trip.

And there was more training to come. Due to the tough conditions, they had to be physically and mentally fit. So, along with the rest of her team, Emma completed an intense physical training course that included camping, rope work, abseiling and other vital skills.

Emma was already a very experienced diver, but she needed special diving training because ice diving was a whole new level of danger. To join the Antarctic team, Emma had to undertake three weeks of additional training. They would be wearing special **dry suits** and equipment which she had to learn how to use properly.

Wetsuits used for normal diving are designed to keep you warm but not dry.

Dry suits are completely sealed and designed to keep all water out, but you need to wear layers of clothing underneath to keep you warm.

If Emma dived under the ice without proper preparation she could die in as little as 10 minutes. If she fell in the water without her special dry suit she would lose the ability to control her limbs within two minutes! She paid very close attention to everything her instructors said.

Only advanced divers were allowed to do the Tasmanian-based diving course, and 90% of commercial divers were men so even the smallest diving suit was way too long. Emma had to put on a belt and fold the excess of the suit over it like a Santa stomach.

They were instructed on how to operate the dry suit and how to deal with possible emergencies. The equipment for ice diving was different too so she had to learn how to use that as well. Although Emma knew the training was necessary, it wasn't a fun experience diving in the bitterly cold Tasman Sea in the middle of winter. Still, it wouldn't be as cold as Antarctica.

After the three weeks' intensive training, Emma was exhausted but ready for the trip. Now all she needed to do was pack.

Then, it was finally time to say goodbye to her family and friends and climb on board the ship that would take her to Antarctica for her three-month scientific adventure.

16

The edge of discovery

There was a buzz of excitement on the ship as it left Hobart, departing on its journey to Antarctica. Emma couldn't believe it was actually happening. It wasn't the first expedition for Kate, the passenger next to her and as she spoke about her experiences in Antarctica, Emma's excitement mounted. After almost six days at sea, she saw her first glimpse of an iceberg. She was standing on the bridge of the ship and there were celebrations all round.

'Wow, that's incredible!' she exclaimed.

Kate nodded. 'It is, isn't it?'

'It's so much hillier than I expected,' Emma exclaimed in wonderment.

The iceberg was as tall as an eight-storey building and the size of four football fields across. It moved slowly and silently across the sea.

A few days later everyone on board was excited to glimpse a little rocky outcrop with some coloured buildings. Emma marvelled at the brilliant white ice and clear blue skies that she could see for miles.

'It's not always like that,' said Kate. 'Blizzards can hit at any moment and reduce visibility to zero.'

Emma was glad it was a clear day so she could enjoy the brilliance of Antarctica.

Rugged up in her **thermals**, outer waterproof clothes, thick red jacket and wool lined beanie, Emma clambered onto a small boat that took her from the ship to the shore. Even though she'd dressed for the weather, it was so cold outside that it took her breath away.

As she took in the stunning scenery all around, Emma couldn't stop smiling. She had made it to

Antarctica. This trip would be really life changing.

They were ushered quickly onto a bright blue bus called a Hagglund that was built to drive on ice and snow.

'They make things eye-catching around here,' said Emma.

Kate laughed. 'The transports really stand out on a clear day, don't they?'

'Sure do.' Emma grinned.

'Unfortunately, as I mentioned, the weather isn't always like this.'

Kate pointed to the clear blue sky. 'That's why all the vehicles are so colourful. So you can see them when the weather's bad.'

The bus had massive black caterpillar wheels to stop it from skidding on the slippery ice, but even so, Emma was nervous.

'I hope the driver knows what he's doing.'

'He sure does,' Kate replied. 'He drove us around on our last expedition. He's an old hand at this. No slope is too slippery for Tod.' She grinned at Emma.

Emma was glad she had goggles to protect her from the glare and she was grateful for Tod's experience when the bus struck a particularly slippery patch. It slid sideways but Tod managed to keep it under control.

The bus took Emma and her group across the ice to their base at Casey Research Station which seemed bigger in real life than the pictures Emma had seen. It looked like a giant red shipping container, perched on the edge of the massive Antarctic ice cap near the rocky Windmill Islands. There are more than 50 islands in the group and tens of thousands of birds live on them. It was the ideal location for scientists like Emma wanting to observe the bird, marine and plant life of this great continent. Kate had told Emma about the giant moss beds around Casey and Emma couldn't wait to see them for herself.

Everyone had been assigned a **donga**, a temporary transportable home to live in and all the dongas were inside the huge red shed that also housed a medical clinic, lounge and dining areas. Emma's donga was situated just outside the main living quarters which she shared with another woman who was the lead scientist on the station. There were other buildings at Casey too – blue, yellow and green sheds – all especially built for scientific research.

Emma liked the friendly, upbeat atmosphere of the base straightaway. The scientists who were already there were pleased to see new faces and even though they were all in a dangerous, unpredictable environment, there was an air of optimism and excitement. There was also great **camaraderie** onsite and everyone happily helped each other and contributed to the day-to-day running of the station. A roster assigned them all duties for the week, and Emma took her turn at vacuuming the living areas, shovelling snow and helping out the chef in the kitchen.

She couldn't wait to get out into the field but there was a lot of preparation to be done first and sites to be picked out. She did extra 'survival' field training and had fun sleeping outside in a rectangular hole in the snow that she dug for herself. The stars were so beautiful when there were no other lights around.

Emma learnt how to use a snow pick to stop herself falling down crevices and how to navigate with a compass that did not point to the same 'south' as was on the map. She learnt that true magnetic south was not exactly at the South Pole but had wandered about a bit. So her compass pointed to magnetic south and the reading had to be adjusted each time she used it so that she could trace her path back to the station.

In spite of the harsh and cold conditions, there was an abundance of bird life and Emma loved watching birds soar through the clear blue sky. Each year albatrosses, petrels, gulls and terns arrived in Antarctica to breed around the rocky coastline and offshore islands.

Casey station was close to a colony of snow petrels, and she loved seeing the pure white birds flying effortlessly back to their chicks who were hidden in small caves amongst the boulders. It was also home to seals and penguins who didn't seem at all bothered by the scientists around them. The penguins were particularly entertaining as they followed each other around and often fell over. So graceful underwater but so clumsy on land.

With her thermals and special clothing, Emma was well prepared for the cold, but it still took her breath away sometimes, so she was amazed one day to see a seal lie down for a sleep on the **fast ice**.

The blue ice bus was too big to manoeuvre around rocks and crevasses and in and out of small spaces.

To get around the base and go on field trips, their transport was a snowmobile pulling a plastic sled on which they placed their research equipment. Sometimes they went cross-country skiing around the base. It was a good way to get exercise and see the local area. As it was summer, the sun didn't actually set – it doesn't go below the horizon – so Emma enjoyed long evenings with spectacular 'sunsets' that lasted for hours and hours.

She quickly discovered that the extreme cold made her very hungry. Fresh fruit and vegetable deliveries were rare because they were delivered by ships that took days to get to Antarctica and only visited the station in summer. So most of the food was frozen, dried or tinned. Emma didn't mind what she ate, just as long as it kept her warm.

It didn't take her long to get used to life in Antarctica, but there was still one hurdle to overcome – her first ice dive.

17

Under the ice

The night before her first dive, Emma's mind raced. Antarctica was such a dangerous and unforgiving place. Any lapse of concentration could lead to serious injury or death. She would have to keep her wits about her.

She was almost as familiar with her equipment now as she was driving her own car. She would have to check each piece methodically so that she could be confident that everything would perform in the way it was meant to.

'You know what you're doing,' she told herself as she tried to drift off to sleep.

'You've trained for this moment. You're as prepared as you'll ever be.'

Next morning, she had to force breakfast down. She needed the energy, but nerves made it hard for her to swallow. There were so many risks in ice diving, like frostbite and hypothermia. And if the ice moved, she could become trapped. One mistake and she could die under the ice. Emma tried not to think about that, instead trying to focus on the experience, which Kate had promised her would be amazing.

Her diving suit was bright red and made from waterproof, breathable nylon. It had black waterproof rubber seals at the neck and wrist and sock seals at the feet to prevent moisture and cold from getting in. Underneath she would wear thermals.

When it was finally time to gear up, Emma's stomach churned, and her legs shook as she prepared her dry suit, checking for air leaks, making sure the exhaust valve was operational and the inflation buttons worked. Next, she applied special lubricant to the zippers and tried them several times to make sure they opened and closed fully.

The team jumped on the boat and drove out to the edge of the sea ice.

Kate was one of the surface team who also helped the divers prepare. After Emma slipped on the dry suit, Kate helped her close the back zip and put the headdress on properly, making sure it was tucked into the neck flap so that everything was properly sealed against the water and cold.

'That feel okay?' she asked.

Emma nodded.

Kate helped her slip on special three-finger gloves that were designed to hold Emma's fingers together so that her hands stayed warm in the freezing water.

Everything was checked and rechecked, including the long cord that would supply Emma with air and be her link to the surface. There was also the communication cable and another strong cord for tethering so that she could be pulled up in an emergency or if she became disorientated under the ice, which was something that could easily happen.

The dry suit felt gigantic. She slipped on a weight belt, a buoyancy compensator vest, an emergency tank of air, additional weights, fins and a bright yellow full-face mask that covered her nose and mouth. The mask had a cord attached that would allow her to speak to Kate back on the surface.

The kit weighed so much that it made it difficult for Emma to move on land, let alone ice. Kate helped her walk so that she wouldn't slip over. Her legs felt like jelly and her heart was racing, but knowing she needed to keep a cool head, Emma forced herself to slow her breathing.

She was used to diving in oceans where it didn't matter if you were a bit off course when you popped back up to the surface. That was definitely not the case for ice diving, though – there was only one way in and one way out. So, she would have to keep her bearings and constantly check for small icebergs that might catch the cord that supplied her air and drag her away underwater. At least they were diving in pairs and the other diver, Ric, had done this many times before.

Emma and Ric sat on the edge of the hole before carefully lowering themselves into water that looked like an ice slushy.

She was hit straightaway with the intense cold that was beyond anything she'd ever felt, but at the same time, an instant sense of freedom from the weight of her equipment. It took her eyes a while to adjust to the lighting, but then she started to relax and enjoy the experience. The water was stunningly clear, but quite dark as they swam away from the boat and under the ice. As the bubbles started to clear, Emma focused on how it felt in that moment. She could feel her toes and inside her suit she was still surprisingly warm. She knew that if she weren't wearing her dry suit, she wouldn't have been able to move her limbs after only two minutes under the ice.

The beauty of life under the Antarctic ice quickly helped Emma to forget her fear. There were fields of fan worms glowing and waving in the water like poppies in the dark. Her torch was like the beam of lighthouse revealing the beauty of this remote world. There was so much more to see here than she'd expected. And she was surprised to note that the marine life was surprisingly similar to what she'd observed in warmer waters. She kicked her flippers and dived down to get a closer look at a colourful sea spider. The floor of the ocean was covered with large basket-shaped anemones and a

penguin shot past her leaving a trail of tiny bubbles from its feathery tail.

The marine life in Antarctica is older than in other parts of the world as many of the predators, including humans, who hunt in warmer waters are not found in this icy climate. So everything seemed bigger here. She saw a giant sponge that she judged from its size must have been around 200 years old. Emma smiled to herself. She was probably the first human it had ever encountered. It was so amazing to be witness to things that no other living person had seen. Here there was nothing to threaten life forms like the giant sponge except for humans.

Once she had become accustomed to being under the ice, Emma was able to take in her surroundings more and venture away from the entrance hole. She swam through a forest of giant kelp and marvelled at giant sea stars and sea spiders scattered across the ocean bed.

While Emma was awestruck by the aquatic life under the ice, she and Ric were here to work, to collect specimens and make observations.

After almost an hour under the ice, Emma glanced to the surface at the light streaming through from the edge of the sea ice some distance away, making the water sparkle like a diamond. She had seen the most amazing sights, but her fingers were painful with cold. It was time to head up.

Just as she'd been trained to do, Emma swam slowly upwards, taking a safety stop five metres before the top then gliding up to the surface where she was helped from the water by Kate and one of the other surface crew. Her equipment felt incredibly heavy again. She was helped out of her flippers and the rest of her gear, exhausted but exhilarated.

'Amazing, heh!' said Kate

Emma nodded and grinned. Even though she had been wearing gloves, her hands were like claws from the cold. It took half an hour before she could open them again, and it hurt even to try.

The surface crew marked the spot on their map so they could find their way back there and carry out more scientific exploration in the same area.

*

The three months in Antarctica went faster than Emma expected. There was so much to learn about in this wild, untamed place and Emma discovered new inspiration for her work every day. She was constantly amazed that marine life could thrive in this harsh, but incredible environment. She dived on beautiful **invertebrate gardens** many times but they were so vast that it would take more time and research to determine how big they actually were.

*

While in Antarctica, Emma and her colleagues developed a major theory about how small changes to the duration of the sea ice around the coast determine what lives beneath them. Their research revealed that in areas where the ice sheets remained all through the summer there was never much light and the strange invertebrate gardens could thrive. Unique to Antarctica were large fields of ancient sponges, anemones and fan worms.

But as the seasons changed, so did the light. In winter it was fully pitch black and in summer there was 24 hours of sunlight. Emma observed that where the ice sheets broke out in summer there was a lot more light penetrating underwater, and seaweed forests were more likely to grow underneath the sheets. Only a small change in the length of the sea ice season could be enough to cause a **tipping point** in the ecosystem below.

Together with the other scientists, she collected a great deal of data to understand why these beautiful marine gardens were thriving and if the clean-up had reduced pollution.

With its brilliant sparkle, incredible marine life and untouchability, Antarctica would always hold a special place in Emma's heart. It was no longer as pristine as it had once been, and with tourism and more scientific expeditions to come, the human impact was likely to increase. Something had to be done now.

'Told you that you'd be sad to leave the place,' Kate said as they travelled back to Australia.

'I really hope I get the chance to come back one day,' said Emma.

Kate nodded.

'I worry about climate change,' Emma continued as they headed for home. 'We need to know how vulnerable the sponge beds will be to early break-up of the ice from increased temperatures.'

'Maybe the sponge beds will adapt,' said Kate.

Emma nodded.

'Hopefully, there are deep-sea colonies of these species that might be able to withstand the effects of climate change. But we will still lose these precious underwater gardens if we don't halt and reverse **carbon emissions.**'

*

Emma made sure she had an ongoing connection to Antarctica. She became Deputy Chair of the Antarctic Science Foundation, a group that worked with the Australian Antarctic Division to support world-class scientific research to advance the understanding and protection of the continent.

She also managed a project with more than 30 other scientists, providing research opportunities to PhD students. The focus of her research was around climate change and the way the sea ice was changing and the impact that would have on the environment. The ice breaking up early was going to cause massive trouble not just for the marine life of Antarctica. The rise in water temperature would also bring about changes to plants that lived above the ice in Antarctica, and the effects of melting ice would be felt much further afield as sea levels rose, everywhere.

18

Reef under pressure

Emma's underwater world extended from the icy waters of Antarctica to the Great Barrier Reef that stretches about 2,600 kilometres along the northern coast of Queensland. It is the largest coral reef in the world and covers an area of about **348,000 square kilometres,** larger than the United Kingdom, Holland and Switzerland combined.

In its current form, the Great Barrier Reef is estimated to be around 8,000 years old and is very significant to First Nations people who have lived and fished there for more than 40,000 years. Before the sea levels rose around 7,000 years ago, they lived on what is now the sea floor.

First Nations Owner groups have kept spiritual and cultural connections and stories for thousands of years. They have passed down stories about the rising sea and how the reef was formed. Today, they have authority for Sea Country Management in large areas of the Great Barrier Reef Marine Park.

There are 400 different species of coral, 500 of seaweed, 4,000 of molluscs, 1,500 of fish, 215 species of birds, dugongs and sea turtles living on and around the reef.

A really important thing happened in 1981. The Great Barrier Reef was the first coral reef ecosystem in the world to be recognised as a World Heritage site by **UNESCO**. This means the World Heritage Committee considered that it had 'outstanding universal value and deserves special protection'.

*

Emma had visited the reef many times, swimming with dolphins, fish, marine turtles and all kinds of amazing sea creatures. She loved its deep blue waters and abundant marine life but was afraid for the future of the reef and its inhabitants from global warming. Bleaching, caused by an increase in sea temperatures during unusually hot summers was killing the coral itself but also supports all the sea plants and fish that live on and around it.

In 2016, Emma was appointed to the Great Barrier Reef Marine Park Authority, responsible for the protection and care of the reef. Its role is to develop plans and policies to try and help the reef in the face of climate change and other threats. It aimed to get local councils involved, encouraging them to take ownership for the sustainability of the reef and do what they can to preserve it in their own regions.

Emma's position on the board of the Marine Park Authority was initially for a five-year term, so she was in a hurry to do as much as she could for the reef in that time. Not long after her appointment she was swimming at the reef and what she saw made her stomach churn. Just below the surface, the usually healthy coral had turned a bright fluorescent white, the normal purples, greens and blues completely bleached from it. She felt sick with fear and sadness. The coral, living, breathing sea creatures, were literally dying before her eyes. Just before they died they went a slight iridescent colour as if they were screaming for help. But nobody, not even Emma could save them. It broke her heart.

Right now, scientists estimate that bleaching has destroyed more than half of the shallow-water corals found on the northern region of the reef. Although research has shown the reefs could recover from mass bleaching over 10 to 15 years, scientists predict that as the planet keeps warming, bleaching will occur more frequently.

*

Why is the planet warming? For the last 200+ years, countries around the world have used more and more energy to grow food, travel, build roads and houses, and make products that we buy. The energy we have used for this has mostly come from burning fossil fuels.

This produces carbon dioxide and other green-house gases into the atmosphere that then act like a blanket, keeping the heat close to the planet and increasing the temperature of the oceans, causing marine life to die.

At the same time the human population has been increasing which increases pollution of the environment as well as energy use. Scientists know that we must do everything we can to reduce carbon emissions as fast as possible.

A world first: Scientists know they don't have time to get everyone in the world to reduce carbon emissions fast enough to save the whole reef, so they are doing experiments to see it they can restore some of the damaged sections. Using loose coral fragments, they have attached more than 2,600 coral fragments to a web of 165 hexagonal sand-coated frames on the sea floor, hoping that the live fragments will continue to grow and become a healthy area of living reef. If it works, we might be able to restore small areas of dying reefs around the world. But it's still a big job.

*

Emma Johnston has won lots of awards and recognition for her world-leading work in Marine Ecology, receiving an Order of Australia in 2018,

and recently being appointed Deputy Vice-Chancellor (Research) at the University of Sydney.

She is still passionate about saving the underwater kingdom that has been so much a part of her life since she was a small child learning to swim in Port Phillip Bay before she could even walk.

To help people around the world understand and see for themselves the effect we are having on our oceans and marine life, she has shared her knowledge in documentaries and media appearances. 'Can we save the reef?' is a film showing the damage and threats to the Great Barrier Reef. It has been shown many times and won a national award. You can check it out: www.youtube.com/watch?v=nYXFEfB2Lf8.

Emma also worked on the fabulous BBC/Foxtel series, 'Coast Australia' and the ABC Catalyst series, amongst others.

Her favourite place is still underwater in her amazing other world or just looking at the ocean and feeling the wind in her hair.

Ways we can reduce our carbon footprint and pollution

There are many ways we can reduce our carbon footprint and help our marine life.

1. Grow your own vegetables if you can and eat more of a plant-based diet.
2. If you have space in the garden or on a balcony, you could make a worm farm for composting food scraps. Some schools have gardens with a worm farm or compost for everyone to recycle food scraps. If your school doesn't have one, you could talk about it with other students, your teachers and the principal, to make it a school project.
3. Use less water – take a 3-minute shower and recycle water where possible for the garden or pots.
4. Use a bamboo toothbrush instead of a plastic one which will end up in landfill.
5. Walk or ride a bike instead of taking the car.
6. Try to use less energy by turning off lights that aren't being used and drying clothes outside in the sun instead of using a tumble dryer.
7. Unplug electrical appliances that aren't being used.
8. Talk to your family about switching to renewable energy, like solar, in your home.

9. Use a china plate to cover food in the fridge instead of gladwrap or other plastic.
10. Recycle as much as you can – glass, paper, cardboard and tins – and avoid single-use plastics.
11. Join a local group where you live that plants trees and restores habitats where you can.
12. Use fabric cloths for cleaning instead of wipes that have microplastics that clog our waterways.
13. Get involved in a beach clean-up.
14. Get a group of concerned students together and talk to your teachers and principal about ways to minimise carbon emissions at your school.
15. Write to your local council, businesses and politicians about your concerns and suggest ways they could make changes in the area you live which wouldn't be too difficult to implement. Letters rather than emails are more likely to be taken seriously.

Glossary

- **Algae** – a simple, non-flowering plant found in a moist environment
- **Abalone** – a type of marine snail found on reefs mainly in cold waters. They have a large foot that they use to attach themselves to reefs or rocks, using suction. Their rough, ear-shaped shells protect them from the waves. In some cultures, they are considered a delicacy and were a staple food for some Aboriginal clans in Tasmania and in other areas of southern Australia.
- **Biology** – the study of life and living things that have at least one cell.
- **Bubonic plague** – is a bacteria spread by fleas and human contact. It was the worst pandemic in the history of the world – in 7 years from 1346-1353, it killed between 75-200 million people when the world population was around 360 million.
- **Camaraderie** – mutual trust and friendship between a group of people.
- **Carbon emissions** – carbon dioxide (the gas we breath out!) that escapes into the atmosphere from burning fossil fuels: in cars, planes, ships, industry, etc. In one year almost 4.5 tons of CO2 per person is emitted – but not by each person, of course!
- **Cells** – the building blocks of all living things.

- **Climate change** – long-term change in the Earth's temperature which can cause significant damage to the environment and affect weather patterns.
- **Crustaceans** – sea creatures with four pairs of legs and a segmented body, eg. crabs, lobsters.
- **Discrimination** – when individuals or groups are unfairly treated because of such things as their race/ethnicity, age, gender or social and economic group (class).
- **Donga** – temporary transportable dwelling.
- **Eco concrete** – concrete designed to have a less negative impact on the environment.
- **Ecological research** – studies things like the health, size, eating habits and interactions of a species and its relationships with the environment and other organisms.
- **Fan worm** – a type of worm with feathery appendages. Also known as the feather duster worm.
- **Fast Ice** – ice that doesn't move because it's attached to the coast or sea floor or locked in place by icebergs.
- **Hull** – the body of a boat.
- **Ice sheets** – layers of ice covering large pieces of land for a long period of time.
- **Microbes** – living things that are so small you can't see them without a microscope. Microbes include things like bacteria, viruses, algae and fungi.

- **Molluscs** – have a soft body and live in water or a damp environment and usually have an external shell.
- **PhD** – an abbreviation for Doctor of Philosophy and is a research degree that takes about 4 years of full-time work after a bachelor's degree and an honours or masters degree.
- **Plankton** – are usually very small marine organisms that do not swim but are carried along by the tides and currents and are a food source for many marine plants and animals including some whales.
- **Spinnaker** – a type of sail that fills with wind and balloons out in front of the boat when it's used.
- **The Great Depression** (1929 to around mid-1930s) – a world-wide economic collapse where many banks and businesses closed down. In Australia around 30% of people lost their jobs. At that time there were no unemployment benefits, so families often had to find food wherever they could with fishing, hunting (usually, rabbits), etc. Interesting facts: the famous tourist route, the Great Ocean Road, along the western coast of Victoria, was built by returned soldiers from World War 1 during this time. And the iconic Sydney Harbour Bridge gave thousands of men a job during the Depression too (built between 1924 to 1932).
- **Thermals** – long underwear that you wear under your clothes to keep you warm.

- **Tipping point** – where a small environmental change like a slight increase in sea temperatures and acidity can cause a major coral bleaching that might be permanent death of that coral reef or decades or centuries for it to recover.
- **UNESCO** – United Nations Educational, Scientific and Cultural Organisation. Their mission is to contribute to building a culture of peace through cooperation in education, arts, sciences and culture.
- **USSR** – stands for the Union of Soviet Socialist Republics. It was a Communist federation of 15 states, with Russia the largest and dominant one. It lasted from 1922 to 1991.
- **World Heritage Site** – a natural or human-made site, area, or structure recognised as being of outstanding international importance and therefore it needs protecting. Sites include The Great Barrier Reef, The Pyramids, Kakadu and the Taj Mahal. Sites are nominated and identified by the World Heritage Convention (an organisation of UNESCO).